DESCENT

The Gryphon Series
Resurrection
Part One

Written by

Stacey Rourke

Published by Anchor Group Publishing
PO Box 551
Flushing, MI 48433
Anchorgrouppublishing.com

Cover Design by KD Designs
Editing & Proofing by There for You Editing, Melanie Williams, and Cheree Castellanos

Other Titles by Stacey Rourke:

Gryphon Series

The Conduit
Embrace
Sacrifice
Ascension

The Legends Saga

Crane
Raven
Steam

Stand Alone:
Adapted for Film

I said if the readers wanted it, I would venture back to Gainesboro. To all my fans, this one is for you!

PROLOGUE

Moments Before Celeste Battled the Countess

"When they catch you—and that's a *when* not an if—you tell them you went to smoke form and clung to a Protector who was plane jumping, do *not* mention my name. Understood?"

My lip curled in disgust and a healthy dose of judgment. "It's really *that* easy to break into this joint? Don't tell me stuff like that! It makes me rethink trading my pesky evil streak for my good-guy merit badge."

Terin glanced my way. Red flames burned within her irises like smoldering embers as she hitched one auburn eyebrow in disbelief. "You've been *conformed* for all of ... what, five minutes? I'm not convinced you couldn't be swayed back to your more dominate nature with the promise of a cookie."

"Give me a little credit!" I argued. "It would have to be a really good cookie. With white *and* dark chocolate chips in it."

"Do you want to know how to get there, or continue to listen to yourself talk?" she asked, jabbing her thumb in the opposite direction of my intended target. "Because either way, I'm out of here in about thirty seconds."

"Easy, Vesuvius," I soothed. "Please, bestow your wisdom."

The curvaceous ginger's mouth, which was normally fixed in a stoic frown, twisted to the side as she fought off an almost grin. "That was actually a good one."

I turned my palms skyward and gave her a "well, duh" look.

A blink and any trace of emotion washed away. "See those double doors?"

I followed her raised hand and nodded my confirmation.

Anxious hands trembling, Terin fumbled with the clasp of her plum-colored cloak. Freeing it from the fastener, she let it fall from her shoulders. "Through there you will find another long hallway, identical to this one. The Council Master's office is there, so keep your head down, hood up, and don't dawdle. The hall ends in a T. At its end, turn to the right. The Hall of the Magi is at the end of that hallway. Trust me, even *you* can't miss it."

"I'm not sure I like the implications of that remark. It makes me think you don't believe I have a brain beneath this roguishly handsome façade." My hand brushed her as I took the cloak she offered me and shrugged it up my arms.

"As your friend, I can only hope someday you find someone that is as attracted to you as you are." The grinding of her teeth became visible in her tightly clenched jaw. "Do you have any idea what you're going to say when you get in there?"

Thumbing the lone button of the cloak through its fastener, I let one shoulder rise and fall in a casual shrug. "Would '*make love, not war*' be inappropriate?"

Terin's frown deepened. "Very much so."

"Huh. Guess I'll just have to wing it then." Grinning, I flipped the hood up over my head.

"*Rowan!*" Terin called out the moment I took my first step toward the double doors.

I swiveled back, forcing a confident smirk that contradicted my knotted gut. "What's the matter, Red? Need a hug good-bye?" I teased, tagging on a playful wink.

Ignoring my antics, stress lines etched deep divots between her brows. "As soon as you walk in, head straight to the symbol tiled into the floor and take a knee. Any other posture will be viewed as a threat and they will kill you on the spot."

"Kneel or die. Got it." I jerked my chin in a brief nod.

Her apricot lips parted to say … something. Quickly rethinking it, she clamped them shut again.

"Good luck," she muttered in place of whatever had been plaguing her, and flicked her gaze to the doors in a signal for me to go.

Our history was a deeply weaved one. If she was the last person I ever spoke to, a simple good-bye seemed inadequate.

"You know this makes us even, right?" I mused in lieu of a deep sentiment.

"No." Head shaking, sadness tugged down the corners of her mouth. "We'll never be even, Rowan. You know that."

A brief beat—in which we exchanged looks of mutual understanding—passed, then I turned on my heel and marched off. I didn't have to look back to know Terin vanished. The temperature of the room dropped about ten degrees in her departure. It was all on me.

Fortunately, I worked better solo. No one to wrinkle their noses about my rather questionable ethics—or lack thereof.

Shoes squeaking over the white marble floor, I strode down the hallway, following Terin's instructions carefully. At the chatter of two nearing men, with wide spanned wings tucked in tight behind them, I fixed my stare on the floor. I contemplated unleashing a bit of violence. It was cardio day, and I could use the thrill. Better judgment reminded me that the ruckus could alert others of my presence. I was the fox in Heaven's henhouse. Being caught there was not an option … not yet at least. Opting to play it safe, I concentrated on both men and extended my influence. Whispering directly into their minds—in that fun little way I do—I assured them I was no interest to them in the slightest. They sauntered past without a moment's hesitation. Some people consider themselves cursed by their demonic attributes. I am not one of them. Two thumbs up for mind control!

Now, nothing stood between me and my goal except for my own trepidation. That was one wailing beast I had learned to silence long ago. Outwardly calm hands rose, flipping back my hood. With a determined stride I crossed the remaining distance to the ornate doors marking the entrance to the Hall of the Magi. Filling my lungs, I gripped the hand-carved doorknob; the top half was a gryphon, the bottom a phoenix. Exhaling a cleansing breath through pursed lips, I yanked open the heavy, cherry wood door.

I was prepared to stare my fears in the face.

If necessary, I would offer myself as a sacrifice.

Even flat out begging was not out of the realm of possibilities.

All of this, and more, I would subject myself to … for *her*.

Celeste Garrett—that mahogany haired, hot-head—had somehow wriggled into my blood stream. She was the hero of the people. Be that as it may, what she needed now was for someone to save *her*. Which was *exactly* what I intended to do.

The sounds of my steps padding across the floor echoed through the cavernous hall. Lit only by dim torches lining the perimeter of the room, I was in no way fooled into believing I was alone in the darkness. Energy crackled around me; its intent menacing and predatory. The threat was so palpable in the air I half expected the walls to grow fangs at any moment and swallow me whole.

My shuffling feet found the symbol on the floor just as Terin had described it.

I expected a grand spectacle the moment the toe of my boot crossed the threshold of the mosaic Celtic trinity symbol. It didn't seem a stretch of the imagination for the heavens to open and cast an ethereal light down on he who dared to tread on this hallowed ground. Unfortunately, like in any moments of great despair when I'd prayed to every god imaginable for a bit of divine intervention, I found myself utterly alone. Well, not *alone* in the literal sense of the word …

"Bold move coming here, pirate," the shadows, flickering and dancing across the walls, hissed. "Surely, you know you don't belong. That pit deep in your gut urging you to flee can attest to that."

"Is that what that is?" I queried, my gaze flitted around the room in search of a solid form to focus on. "What a relief. I thought I ate some pad Thai."

From within the densest fog of the inky darkness, a pair of glowing eyes emerged. Each was easily the size of my head. Smoldering lava churned and writhed with the deep vats of those piercing pupils. "It does not respect us. *Insssssssulant wretch*. Perhapsssssss its bones crunching between my beak will provide the needed motivation to adjust its attitude."

"Steady, friend," a baritone deep enough to rattle my ribs murmured from somewhere in front of me.

Bloody darkness, I mentally scoffed. *Is a bit of overhead lighting really* that *hard to install? Even in the Underworld we managed to score a bit of track lighting to get us by.*

"Remember, we still need him." Formidable talons clicked against the marble floor. Darkness birthed forth the imposing presence of the Gryphon.

I've seen many a man's share of beasties in my time, yet still the regal majesty of the creature knocked the breath from my lungs. Avian elegance combined with feline fluidity, drawing on the most prominent attributes of both.

Flaxen feathers across his broad chest ruffled and smoothed. His pointed ears perked in my direction with interest. "An end of days type battle is looming. She, whom you *claim* to care for, is pinned in the eye of that. Yet, here you stand. Tell me, Rowan Wade, what could have possibly torn you from the woman you vowed to protect?"

Taking a brazen step closer, my head fell back to meet his eagle eyes. Squaring my shoulders, my chin jutted forward with determination for my cause. "I want you to release her."

I expected rage—a spontaneous eruption of violence in which the two beasts would pounce and reduce me to chum in a matter of seconds. Instead, the Gryphon cocked his head with a birdlike twitch.

He peered at me thoughtfully, as if reading every trouble scrawled on my heart. “You know, then, what she must do?”

“No! I know what *you’re* making her do!” I erupted, my hands balling into tight fists at my sides. “She’s your Conduit. Your prop. You are holding her here when what she *should* be doing is running like hell to the farthest reaches of this sodding planet where the likes of you and your kind can never find her again!”

“You think such a place exists? More importantly, you think her capable of that? Of running from her calling and those who depend on her?” The Gryphon matched my step with one of his own, inching himself farther into the light. His firm yet patient tone reminded me of a parent scolding a fussing toddler.

Maybe that’s exactly what I was when it came to her: weak and vulnerable like a babe.

“No, she would never do that. But I have a feeling your influence could be to blame,” I growled, allowing accusation to drip from my tone.

If the Gryphon noticed my deliberate insolence, he chose to ignore it. “I’m sorry, son. Her warrior spirit was there long before our bond was forged. That’s a part of who she is. I would wager it also ranks as one of the reasons you love her.”

“I am not your son!” The words gushed from my lips, fast and furious; my tongue purging my troubled soul. “And I am not leaving here until you *sever that sodding bond!”*

"Yes, you are, Rowan." The firmness of his statement left no room for negotiation. "Because that is a request I *can*not, and will not, honor."

"Even though you know what it could cost her?" As I jabbed an accusing finger at his barrel chest, I felt the temperature of the room spike—the Phoenix flaring in defense of his friend.

"She won't make it out of this alive!" I bellowed.

A menacing hiss snaked along the wall behind me. The air shifted, heat from the Phoenix stalking steadily closer.

The Gryphon craned his neck to the side, his beak snapping for his cohort to stand down. By the time he glanced back, his mask of neutrality was fixed firmly in place. "You are not the only one that cares for her. Trust that if there was another option, I would eagerly pursue it. Unfortunately, such a miracle does not exist. Not yet at least."

Each drum of my pulse pounding in my temples chipped away at the hope I had been clinging to. "There has to be another way." Even I heard the anchor of defeat in my tone, sinking it to the depths of despair.

"There *is* no other way!" The ground shook beneath my feet with the Gryphon's first heated shout. The dominance asserted in his thundering roar would make the most ferocious of beasts cower at his feet.

For a beat, I merely stared, my tongue flicking across my lower lip. Then, with a laugh lacking in humor, I let my chin fall to my chest. Thumbing the clasp free, I allowed the cloak to drift to the floor in a pile at my feet.

"Well," stepping free of the pooled fabric, I rolled my shoulders and shook out my arms, "I said I wasn't leaving without you cutting ties, and I meant it. Looks like your hot-headed friend with his charcoal-scented body odor will get his wish. We're gonna have to tangle, boys."

The Phoenix threw his wings out wide, his flames reaching for the ceiling like malicious claws. "No weapon, no plan, no hope," he snarled, and snapped his beak hungrily.

"Oh, there's a plan." I raised my fists in my best impression of Bert Lahr's Cowardly Lion. "I plan to get in a few good swings that will, at the very least, bruise your larynx as you swallow me whole. I'll be dead, but you'll be on a liquid diet for a few days. Who's *really* the loser there, huh?"

Air leaked past the Phoenix's fangs, slow and deadly, in anxious anticipation.

"No!" the Gryphon rumbled. "Only by drawing strength from all those she holds dear will the Conduit stand even a glimmer of a chance at survival! I hold a deep affection for that girl. Whether you like it or not, I *will* see to it that you are by her side. Not for your own selfish desires, but because she *needs* you!"

The tendons in my neck bulged to the point of pain. A crimson haze of fury seeped in around the edges of my vision. "*You care for her so deeply you would sentence her to death*?"

"You speak of things you can't begin to understand!" the Gryphon countered.

My contest to the contrary was forming on my lips when the Gryphon threw back his head. Throat bobbing, he emitted four high-pitched squawks to the ceiling.

The fur along his hackles rose, soothing as the intensity of his stare returned to me. "Your escorts to lead you *out* will be here soon. They're known for being a bit rough with those that enter the hall uninvited. My suggestion? Leave before they arrive."

"You too big a coward to handle me yourself?" I glowered.

In a blur of speed and a ruffle of feathers, the Gryphon towered over me, the heat of his breath tossing the hair from my brow. "I want you gone, not dead. However, the longer you are here, the more likely I am to alter that particular agenda."

The Phoenix huffed his approval at the idea of my bloody demise.

The tension filled moment was interrupted by the hall doors crashing open. Three burly looking men—poster boys for illegal muscle enhancers—stormed in. While both the Gryphon and the Phoenix retreated to the shadows, the steroid brothers circled me.

"Clearly you boys don't know who you're dealing with." Tilting my head, I let my influence vine into the weak minds of my would-be attackers. Their steps slowed. Their foreheads puckered as my will overpowered theirs with ease.

Tossing the hair from my eyes, I scoffed. "It seems you underestimated the range of my—*huunnh*!"

I didn't see the stealthy fourth newcomer to our little party until his volleyball-sized fist slammed into my face. The power in his punch snapped my head to the side and spun me like a top. Black blood gushed from my nose, dripping off my chin.

"For a moose of a lad, you are impressively light on your feet." Giving praise where praise was due, I wiped at my nose with the back of my hand. "Now, as you are between me and my objective, I'm going to have to ask you to dance out of the way, twinkle toes."

"That's not going to happen," the mammoth of a man rumbled.

"Pity, that." I shrugged and drove my fist fast and hard into his kidney.

Breath was forced from his lungs in a painful wheeze. A regular bloke would've needed a moment to collect himself after such a strike; however, this mammoth beast needed no such pause. His glare set with murderous intent, he lashed out in two quick jabs that rocketed in before I could raise an arm to block. Strike one collided with my cheek bone in an explosion of white, hot radiating pain. The second connected just beneath my eye socket, snapping my head back and making black spots dance before my eyes. My head fogged enough to release those under my control. That was all it took. In an instant I was surrounded, my arms pinned behind me.

"Halt! Hold him steady," the Gryphon commanded and stalked into the midst of the mayhem. "You have overstayed your nonexistent welcome, Rowan. Now, you're needed back in Gainesboro." His wings arced wide behind him, then curled in until the tips of his ivory feather tickled across my forehead.

Light flashed, and I was gone.

I swirled and bobbed as an eddying black wisp of smoke, unsure of where I was or where I was going. The sensation was strangely familiar to the time I rummed myself into a stupor and woke up in a wave pool. Slamming against the sides over and over, I was certain I had found myself flushed in a giant toilet.

Her voice came to me as a beacon through the storm of chaos. My true north, guiding me home.

"I think so," Celeste snarked to Terin, fiddling with her bothersome bangs, which had fallen in her eyes.

Unaffected by the prospect of interrupting them, I wrapped the ghostly mist that *would* be my hand around Celeste's wrist.

Despite herself, I saw a bemused smirk tug at the corner of the fated warrior's lips. "And if I can't, *he* can," she tacked on to a conversation I couldn't have cared less about.

What dire issue I was interrupting mattered shockingly little. That moment was my last chance to reason with her. She could've been giving her confession to the Pope, and I still would have cut in, with no apology. Letting my form swirl in close, I teased across the back of her neck.

Giving a throaty chuckle at the chill that forced her shoulder blades together, I sighed against the nape of her neck, "A word, please?"

Before she could argue, I enveloped her in my cool mist and transported her a few feet away in our conjoined cloud of smoke.

Through experience, I anticipated her reaction: the greenish pallor, profuse sweating, and surly disposition that would follow. However, the army of demons that spun on me, eager to attack if she so much as batted an eye, was a new and exciting development.

"It's okay!" Celeste raised one hand to steady them. The other planted on her knee as she attempted to breathe through a wave of vertigo. “I’m fine. He’s a friend—in a *very* liberal use of that word. So, as you were, stand down, or whatever command means ‘chill the crap out.’ ”

Shaking my head in disbelief, I watched what appeared to be roughly two hundred demons, of varying levels of nastiness, obey her command without question.

“Because why *wouldn’t* she come back from a solo day out with an army of loyal demon followers?” I snorted with a wry huff of laughter.

Only Celeste Garrett could achieve such a feat … it was all part of the annoying wonder that was she.

Wiping the clammy sweat from her brow, Celeste rose to her feet. Her chestnut eyes flicked over my face, taking in every bruise and sizing up every gash. “Squeeze in one last cage match before the apocalypse, did ya?”

“It seems we don’t have one iota of self-preservation between us.” I rolled my jaw to loosen the muscles that were tightening beneath my bruised cheek.

“Rowan, are you—”

Adamantly, I shook my head before she could turn this around on me. If I let this be about me for even a second, my selfish nature would demand I whisk her out of there mid-blink and deal with the consequences later. Stepping in close enough for my chest to brush the sharp points of her breasts, desperation dropped my voice to a rough gravel. “I get that you’ve accepted yourself as the sacrificial lamb, but I haven’t. I meant what I said about standing beside you to the end. I *will* lay down my life before I see any harm come to you. No matter what. But if I thought for one minute you'd go willingly, I'd transport you to the ends of the earth where none of this could ever find you."

Deep within the warm molasses pools of her eyes lingered a flicker of doubt. Somewhere within her, in the darkest crevices of her mind she dare not speak of, lay the normal girl who longed to break free from all of this. I could see it in the catch of her breath and the gleam of endless possibilities that softened her furrowed brow.

Forcing her gaze from mine, she glanced around at the evacuated town. That was all it took. The willful fire raged in her soul once more; its inferno straightening her spine, and adding a firm set to her jaw.

Gently she laid her hand to my cheek, empathically offering me a hint of her resolve. Her face telling more than her borrowed emotions ever could. Still, I welcomed the gift of her touch.

"I *have* to do this," she explained, smiling softly as I leaned into her palm. "I hope you can understand."

Without another word, or second glance, Celeste spun on her heel and stalked toward her awaiting army.

"It's almost dusk," she commanded in a stern bellow. "Those that are coming will be here soon. The rest of you, *fall in line*."

As a lump of resentment rose in my throat, I watched her walk away. With the clarity of absolute truth, I realized she was lost to me ... without the pleasure of ever having her at all.

CHAPTER 1

Eight months and one universal brain bleaching later ...

"You're a villain," Celeste breathed the words against my lips in a throaty whisper. "A scoundrel. A complete ..."

"Dick?" I offered, kissing and nibbling my way down her neck to the enclave above her collarbone.

Many a fantasy of mine played out as she wove her hands into my hair, guiding my mouth back to hers. "I was going to say rascal," she giggled. "You *know* I have a paper on examples of feminism in contemporary art due Friday. Yet here you are, distracting me with your magic tongue and pelvic wizardry."

"Of all my sins, I can't even *pretend* to repent for that one." Diving into her kiss, I eagerly lost myself in the nirvana of her touch.

Celeste rolled her hips beneath me, eliciting an animalistic growl that tore from my throat. The intimate touch of a Conduit was a heady tonic, one I had quickly formed an addiction to.

Now, I know what you're thinking. *Wait, what? Rowan isn't supposed to have any memories of their life beforehand! How can he recall her true calling? What is that devilish handsome rapscallion up to?*

That's the part where I truly am I wanker.

Maybe it was my mind control ability. Maybe I was a beacon of iron clad resolve. Whatever the reason, I remembered ... *everything*. From my first taste of the fabled Conduit of the Gryphon, to when she saved me from a near fatal knife wound. I recalled it all in vivid detail: our spats, our flirtations, and our disharmony over me selling her out to an army of evil gnomes. Why didn't I speak up and clue her in to her true calling?

My compassionate reasoning? Here, she was happy. The fate of the world wasn't balancing on her petite shoulders. She laughed. She joked. She enjoyed life as a normal young woman.

My selfish motives? With her memories restored she would return to barely tolerating me. Most definitely she wouldn't let my hand wander under the airy fabric of her cotton T-shirt to enjoy the velvety skin beneath as I was right then. Stifling a moan, the tips of my fingers brushed over the lacework of scars lining her midsection. To her, they were reminder badges of childhood illnesses. I considered them more the Braille *War and Peace* narrative of every battle she had ever fought. Curling my hand around her slender waist, I drew her close enough to feel the thump of her heart pounding in her chest. Lips crushed together with mutual intensity, a low groan rumbled from my chest. In moments like this, I couldn't even pretend to feel guilty for all I was keeping from her.

Sliding her knee to the side, she granted me access to wriggle into the tempting V of her denim-clad thighs. Self-serving cad that I was, I knew enough about Celeste Garrett to manipulate my way into her good graces. I, more than anyone, knew what a vile and unspeakable betrayal that was. Still, what had blossomed between us since then was real. So much so that I would protect her, and the fragile ecosystem of her new life, with my dying breath.

With nightmarish visions of destiny catching up to her playing behind my eyes, I pulled back. Pushing up to sit, I stared into her chestnut eyes, mesmerized by the tiny flecks of gold which swirled and danced within. That squinty-eyed look she used to get whenever she wanted to punch me in the face was gone. All that lingered now was an intoxicating blend of acceptance, affection, and desire.

Lower lip jutting out in a delectable pout, her hand traced the line of my jaw. "Wow, you look really bummed. Am I that bad at this? You know what, don't answer that. That said, if you would rather thumb wrestle, I would totally understand."

Chuckling, I leaned in to press my forehead to hers. Her silken hair tickled my skin in a way that made it come alive at the electrifying touch. "My mind wandered off for a minute. I wrangled it back."

Palms pressed to my chest, she playfully pushed me away. Sitting up, she straightened her disheveled shirt. "Because that's what all girls like to hear when their boyfriend is cresting Mt. Boobage. Way to kill the mood, Casanova."

"No, no, no," I encouraged, attempting to ease her back down on the frightfully lumpy dorm mattress. "No pulling back down of clothes! Possibly taking them clean off and staying in bed! All thoughts were of you, I swear it."

"Oh yeah?" she jabbed, one brow raising in question. "Prove it. Tell me exactly what you were thinking, and make it convincing, or the shoes are going back on, too."

"I was thinking ..."

That this is all fleeting. That one simple memory being triggered is all it will take to tear you away from me. That if the truth ever does *come out, you will never look at me the same again—and most likely you'll hate me enough to kill me for it.*

"... that I love the way you look at me." In desperation, I grabbed for one truth in the sea of lies I had cast myself into.

Tilting her head with a wry smirk, chestnut bangs fell into her eyes. "Rowan Wade, a sappy romantic. What will the other girls on campus say? A secret this big gets out and it could *totally* destroy your reputation."

"I trust you'll be discreet," I countered, feigning a somber frown.

"Heck, no!" She laughed, and flopped back on her pillow. "I'm printing off fliers and covering the quad with them."

"Sodding minx!" Pouncing, I tickled the spot below her ribs that made her snort in an unbecoming way I found absolutely adorable.

Blood beginning to pump with the prospect of our playful tussle turning into naughty fun time, I audibly groaned my disappointed when the door burst open and Celeste's roommate, Terin, sauntered in.

One look at our tangled limbs, and a cat-that-ate-the-canary grin twined across her face.

"Whatcha doin'?" the curvaceous redhead asked with a saucy wink.

I should've been annoyed by her busting in, and timing wise I absolutely was. However, Terin, aka the fiery Conduit of the Phoenix, and I had developed a three-century old habit of saving each other from dismal fates. I knew her as the straight-laced champion for good she had been *before* the memory wipe turned her into a binge drinking party girl straight out of Girls Gone Wild Co-Ed edition. The ironic merit of her alter ego alone was priceless.

Face blooming a bright tomato red, Celeste shoved me off of her and sat up to comb her fingers through her hair. "Nothing! We weren't doing anything."

Kicking off a pair of wedge sandals, Terin swapped them out for flip flops. "Nothing looks shockingly similar to achieving third base."

Flopping back down on the bed behind Celeste, I laced my fingers behind my head. "Did you not see the sock on the door, po—pet?" By far the hardest part of the whole mind-meld façade was curbing my impulse for pirate slang. "Or did you just assume that the contraption was cold and in need of a hat?"

Celeste's head whipped around, her eyes bulging with mortified shock. My rabid little tea-cup poodle … "*You put a sock on the door*? We only came in here because you said you wanted to borrow a sweatshirt!"

"That's code for nookie, lovee. Everyone knows that." I grinned. My gaze slowly traveled the length of her, taking the leisurely route to linger over all the curves.

"Oh, yeah. Everyone knows that." Terin lifted one shoulder casually and let it fall. Snatching a duffle bag from beside her bed, she unzipped it and sniffed the articles of clothing stuffed inside. Cringing, she discarded them onto the floor.

"You're staying then?" I ventured. "Would that be in an observation or active participation roll?"

Without turning around, Celeste slapped blindly behind her. Her hand cracked against my upper thigh with a loud clap. Wincing, I stifled a whimper. She might not remember being the Chosen One, but she still packed a supernatural wallop.

"Don't you have class, like, right now?" my delicate little flower asked her roomie.

"All classes have been canceled. The rumor is they found a girl dead in the quad." Stuffing clean-ish clothes back into her bag, Terin's tone seemed oddly disconnected, considering the subject matter.

"*What*?" Springing off the bed, Celeste's hands instinctively balled into tight fists at her side. "We have to go! We need to find out ..."

Sentence trailing off, confusion creased her brow. For a moment her warrior nature clawed its way to the surface. Even so, her cleansed mind had no clue what to make of the impulse.

"Find out what, pet?" Pushing myself up on one elbow, I bristled with fear in anticipation of her response.

Celeste's stare flicked my way, bewilderment and desperation sharpening her features. Her heart-shaped lips opened and shut, yet couldn't form a single word.

"Hate to ruin your fun, Nancy Drew, but I don't think there's much of a mystery to solve here," Terin scoffed. Zipping her bag shut, she tossed it over her shoulder. "Most likely a small town freshman got a taste of freedom, but forgot to learn when to say when. Poor thing probably drank herself to death. Now, I'm going into town to hit a yoga class. You two can get back to your regularly scheduled afternoon delight." Flicking her ponytail over her shoulder, she sashayed from the room and pulled the door shut behind her.

Celeste stared after her without blinking. With an exasperated sigh, I rolled off the bed and thumbed the buttons of my shirt closed. Whatever enticing plans I may have had for the day were squashed by the troubled expression carved on her face. If I wanted to keep her white-washed mind protected, I would have to show her there was nothing for her to do, and no one for her to save. Here, she was free. Her heroic nature could rest, and I would move angelic realms and the Underworld both to keep it that way.

"Since I've lost your attention completely, how about if we go see what the coconut telegraph has to say about the campus drama?" I offered with a tight-lipped smile.

A small part of me wanted her to argue, as if such a contention could offer an iota of proof that she could overcome her true nature for the long haul.

Much to my disappointment, she started for the door without looking back. "I have to know ..." she murmured, and vanished down the hall at a steady trot.

Cursing under my breath, I jogged to catch up.

"Well this is not a boat accident," I whistled through my teeth, quoting the infamous line from *Jaws*. "You don't get a turn out like this for simple alcohol poisoning."

Cop cars, paramedics, and fire trucks surrounded the campus, all with their lights flashing. The center court of the quad was blocked off with yellow crime scene tape. News crews peppered the area, all in the midst of their on-air coverage of the events unfolding. It seemed everybody on campus, except for the yoga bound Terin, had ventured out to gawk at the spectacle. Milling through the swarming crowd, we were elbowed and jostled between strangers, but made no real headway toward a better vantage point.

Lacing her fingers with mine, Celeste jerked her chin in the direction of a narrow alley that ran between the dining hall and one of the dorms. "We can get through up there." Using her small frame to weave through the crowd, she dragged me along behind her.

Shimming down the length of the elegant stone aisle, we spilled out right in front of the quad. The yard, which was normally scattered with lounging students—and a seemingly endless game of Hacky Sack—had been completely blocked off, strobing with red and blue lights. Two men in black uniforms lifted a body bag, complete with cargo, onto a gurney and rolled it to the back to their coroner's van. A detective, pen and pad posed and ready, questioned three frantic looking lasses. Judging by their red-rimmed eyes and dripping noses, they either knew the victim or found the body.

"Excuse me, Officer!" Celeste called to the middle-aged, plain clothes cop that stalked passed. He had the flattened nose of a former boxer, and the surly disposition to match. "Does anyone know what happened here?"

Pausing mid-stride, his hands fell limp at his sides, annoyance sagging his shoulders. "Yeah, I've ignored the million questions asked by all the other kids. But for *you*, I'll stop what I'm doing—you know, trying to actually *solve* the crime—and fill you in on all the details," he snapped irritably.

"S-sorry, to bother you," Celeste stammered, self-consciously pulling back at his response.

I spent centuries in the Underworld where fellow demons would torture and fillet each other simply as a form of Friday night entertainment. But this guy? He was needlessly nasty. It was with great pleasure that I tipped my head and let the fingertips of my influence turn him into my obedient little sock puppet.

Turning our way on the ball of his foot, the officer suddenly offered us a warm and friendly smile. "I am terribly sorry. That was an incredibly rude and unnecessary way for me to behave toward an obviously concerned citizen. I would gladly answer any questions you may have to the best of my ability."

Smile glued in place, he stood blinking in eager anticipation of our requests.

A bit over the top? Probably. That didn't make it any less funny.

"Uhh ..." Celeste shot a sideways glance in my direction, her nose crinkling in confusion.

Marveling at how she made even open-mouthed stupefaction look adorable, all I could do was shrug as if I was equally baffled.

"What can you tell us about what happened?" Celeste ventured, keeping her tone level and words carefully measured.

"Oh, her?" Plunging his hands into the pockets of his slacks, the jovial officer rocked back on his heels. "The victim spent last night doing a bar crawl with her friends. Around midnight they lost sight of her. This morning a student from Glassell Hall went for a jog and found her body. Before arriving on the scene, the fellas and I thought for sure this would be a drug or alcohol induced incident. Then, we got here and found her propped up on one of the benches.

Poor thing was sitting pretty with her legs crossed and hands folded in her lap, like she was waiting on a bus. That ruined our theory for me. I have spent enough time in gin-induced blackouts to know they *never* end that pretty. It's usually a sprawled out mess of drool and self-loathing. Hell, that's why my wife left me after seventeen years." Pausing, his eyebrows pinched tight. "Not sure why I just told you that ..."

Something about the precise positioning of the body unleashed a serpent of unease that slithered up my spine. "What about the body? Were there signs of a struggle?"

"None at all." The officer shrugged, the thick paunch of his mid-section straining against the buttons which held the hard-working fabric closed. "Our guys couldn't find a thing wrong with her! She had no external injuries, her airway was open and clear, and judging from the toxicity report, she must have been last night's designated driver. Cause of death is completely undeterminable at this point." Stabbing his hands onto his hips, he screwed his lips to the side. "Isn't this a pickle of a case?"

"Sh-should you be telling us all the details?" Celeste stuttered, glancing around to see who—if anyone—was listening. Luckily, the alley was clear of further vagabonds.

"Probably not," our new friend admitted with a mischievous wink.

My teeth ground to the point of pain as I ticked through the various brands of nastiness that could kill without any signs of physical trauma. A single thought made my blood run cold. I didn't want to speak the words, hated to ask the question out of sheer fear of the answer.

"Did she have any tattoos?" I forced the words through clenched teeth.

"Now that you mention it, she did!" Officer Mind-puppet chirped.

Delving deeper into his mind, I pushed. "What did it look like?"

Pulling a pen from his breast pocket, he extended his hand to Celeste. "May I?"

"Sure," she grimaced, and placed her hand in his, "I always allow strangers with bi-polar mood fluctuations to draw on me."

"Lucky for me!" The officer chuckled, and bent his head to his task. The point of his pen flicked over the delicate skin of her palm at a fevered pace. "This is a rough sketch. Her mark was fancier with all sorts of scrolling and shading. Still, this will give you the gist of it."

Artwork complete, he turned Celeste's hand to present it to us.

"Huh," Celeste muttered, seemingly oblivious the world was spinning around me in a dizzying hodgepodge of looming carnage and gore.

My vision tunneled.

Blood thumped an ominous chorus in my temples.

The mark was a simple one—an X with a circle above it. Be that as it may, I knew of it well. The planted fear of it was deep ... demonic lore.

Lurking somewhere nearby, a Hellhound was loose on the Rhodes campus. It would consume without mercy or bias: human and demon alike. Devouring souls, it would build in strength until it brought first the town, then the world to its knees. If the rumors and warnings of the Underworld were correct, once that symbol appeared, an onslaught of carnage would soon follow. This one dead girl was only the beginning.

CHAPTER 2

"That was weird, right?' Celeste gnawed on her lower lip, her fingertips skimming over the stone wall as we skirted back down the alley. "Cops, as a rule, aren't usually that … forthcoming."

Nudging her shoulder with mine, I peered up at her from under my brow, slathering on the charm. "Spend a lot of time with cops, do you?"

"Do the ones on my favorite crime dramas count?"

"Are those the shows were the guys are all ripped and the ladies look like swimsuit models?"

Celeste raised one finger in a warning. "They are, and before you say another word, you should know you are treading dangerously close to ruining my entire outlook on reality."

"I'll leave you to your delusion then." Catching one lock of her chestnut hair, I gave it a playful tug. "I have to ask, did you find what you were looking for?"

My breath caught in anticipation of her answer, fearing a thread in the intricately woven tapestry of the Counsel's elaborate lie may have snagged.

Her stare fixed straight ahead, focused yet unseeing. I could almost see the warrior hidden beneath her façade of normalcy—lost and unneeded.

"No, I …" Physically she shook herself from the reverie. Yet before she fixed her mask back in place, I caught a glimpse of the true sadness beneath. It caused a hot rush of guilt to inject itself into my veins. "Sorry, we can go. I was just … curious."

Even now, in this new reality, she longed for the hero's life. It was in her blood. If my own yearning to rid her of that burden came to pass, would I treasure her the same?

"Maybe instead of an art teacher you should join the men and women in blue. If for no other reason than handcuff fun." Pushing my own dark ponderings aside, I waggled my eyebrows in case she'd missed the none too subtle come-on.

An impish grin curled across her lips. Casting her gaze down the alley in one direction, then the other, she caught my belt loop with her forefinger and tugged me in close enough for her body to mold to mine. "You know, that sock is still on the doorknob ... unless you feel it would be wasted time without those cuffs?"

I stifled a groan behind my teeth before gently pushing her back and forcing some distance—and space for better judgment—between us. "Believe me when I say there is *nothing* I'd like more. Unfortunately, I have a study group tonight which is vital to me actually *passing* my Economics class," I lied.

Celeste pantomimed shock and slack-jawed awe, her hand fluttering to her face. "These words are foreign from this being. I fear he may be a pod person."

My head fell back in laughter. "Yes, I do actually study. Which, to my great disappointment, means I'm going to have to take a rain check, *mo chroi*." The air was knocked from my lungs at my slip-up. I hadn't dared utter that phrase since the reset button had been pushed on our lives. In Celtic it meant "my heart," and it had been my pet name for her back when our relationship consisted only of emotional angst and frequent throat punches.

Chestnut eyes, swimming with flecks of gold, swung my way. Deep lines sliced between Celeste's brows. "What did you just call me?" Her attempt at a lighthearted laugh bubbled with underlying nerves.

She remembered.

The full caliber of what, I couldn't say. Judging by the bewilderment etched on her face, she was asking herself that same question. Even so, something about the nickname sparked a twinkling of memory. Which could only mean … it meant something to her. As much as she had sworn she loathed me, that phrase stirred something within her. This realization hit me with a puzzling blend of elation and abject terror that the delicate world the Counsel created may already be crumbling.

"I think it's Latin for … something." On a good day, lies rolled from my tongue like melted caramel, meant to sweeten anyone into coming around to my way of thinking. This one soured with a pungent aftertaste. "Must have heard it in a movie or something. I thought it sounded charming … decided to try it out on a susceptible young lass. Hit or miss?"

Her tongue flicked over her front teeth, trying—unsuccessfully—to stifle a smile. "It *might* be a hit, *if* you knew what it meant. For all we know, you could've just called me 'walrus nuts.' "

Catching her hand, I yanked her into my arms. My hands fell comfortably into place around her narrow waist. We stood at the opposite end of the alley, where the masses swarmed the scene. The buzz of chaos threatened to swallow any conversation attempted. "Head back to your room, walrus nuts," I muttered against her ear, so my message didn't get lost. "As soon as I'm done, I'll race up there and we can pick up right where we left off."

"I'm putting in my vote now for that nickname not to stick." She giggled, her lips teasing over mine.

"Noted," sucking air through my teeth, I cringed, "but I fear the motion has already passed."

As I reluctantly pulled myself away from the warmth of her curves, she caught the collar of my shirt and tugged me in close.

"Hurry back," she breathed against my lips. Taunting me with only a dotted kiss to the tip of my nose, she sashayed off. Her ponytail, twitching from side to side, quickly vanished into the sea of bodies.

My heart seized in a tight fist of melancholy the moment she disappeared from sight. She was the first girl I ever wanted to spend more than a long weekend with. The first to make me abandon self-preservation if it meant keeping her safe and content.

I used deception to get close to her.

All of this was a fleeting illusion.

I knew that.

Even so, it was real to me. I was happier and more alive by her side than I had been in centuries. I fully intended to squeeze every grain of sand out of this free-flowing hour glass that counted down to my misery and despair ... unless I could find a way to prevent that. Ducking back down the alley, I dissipated in a cloud of black smoke.

CHAPTER 3

Pool balls clanked together at The Four Seasons Bar, an establishment frequented by demons, imps, and other assorted monsters. The dimly lit watering hole reeked of stale nicotine and bad choices.

Weaving through the marsh of glares and sneers, I easily located my target. She wasn't exactly incognito in her painted on python print pants, thigh-high stilettos, and lace-up leather bodice.

"You went for the more demure look today," I pointed out, leaning one hip against the edge of the pool table. "What happened? Did the neighbor's Rottweiler need his studded collar back?"

Kat, a college girl who had been abducted and demonically infected by my very dead ex-boss, paused from lining up her shot at the nine ball to glower up at me beneath her curtain of stick-straight raven hair. Cleopatra would've ridiculed this girl for her over-use of eyeliner. "Well, well, well, look what washed ashore ... the bad boy pirate gone soft."

Dissolving in a cyclone of smoke, I curled and wisped my way to her side. Solidifying, my hand closed around her pool stick. Before she could so much as blink in my direction, I jammed the chalked end under her chin, applying just enough pressure to make the whites of her eyes swell. "And what, pray-tell, makes me soft? That I haven't killed you yet? That's a prospect which can be *very* easily remedied."

It was desire—not fear—that darkened her eyes to a glowing amber. "There's my boy," she purred, her gaze doing unspeakable things to me. "I do enjoy a good, *dirty* blond. Glad to see your reputation wasn't all hype. That would've ruined the fantasy."

Twirling her stick over the back of my palm, I released it back to her open hand. "I've been with some questionable strumpets, but quite honestly, lass, you frighten me. And not in the fun way."

"Fear can be a powerful aphrodisiac." Her tongue dragged over her lower lip, wiggling the dainty silver ring pierced through her plump flesh.

"As fun as this verbal copulation is, I actually came here for a reason." Breathing through my mouth became mandatory so as to not gag on her potent blend of patchouli oil and musk.

"It's still your shot, Kat," a mocha-skinned bruiser, with milky white eyes and a soft voice that contradicted his gruff appearance, muttered. Crossing his bulging arms over his torso, he stared laser beams of hate my way.

I helped his mood along by blowing him a kiss.

"So, tell me, *pirate*," Kat goaded, "if this isn't a social call, much to my supreme disappointment, what can I do for you?"

"I'm in a bit of a spot and need your help." Running my finger over the edge of the table, I grimaced and wiped the greasy sludge that my digit came away with on my pant leg. "However, this particular task will require your comrades as well. What is it you crazy kids have been calling yourselves? The Mutants of Mayhem?"

Rising to full height, Kat cocked one hip and jammed her fist to it. With one finger she halted the annoyed heaving of her cloudy-eyed friend.

"We are less for hire and more for doing whatever the hell we want, but thanks for the offer," she snorted, her black-painted lips pursed tightly.

Stepping in close, I brushed the hair from her shoulder to murmur against her ear, "Last I heard, you all took a knee and named the Conduit of the Gryphon your leader. Tell me, where is your pint-sized frontrunner now?"

"What do you know, Rowan?" she hissed through her teeth, living up to her feline nickname.

"It can be summed up quite simply, actually." Borrowing her stick once more, I took her shot. The balls met with a sharp clap before the nine slid into the center pocket. "None of you have any idea where she is. Add that to your pack-like mentality, and the lot of you are basically lost souls bumping into each other and wreaking havoc until 'mommy' decides to come back for you. The Macaulay Culkin *Home Alone* vibe is a sad trait in a demon."

My jab shifted the mood of the room. Silence suddenly reigned. A pin drop would have resonated like a scream. Growls seeped from every corner. I had the attention of each and every demon there. The whole outing instantly became infinitely more fun.

Kat glanced around the room, anticipating a bomb strike, yet uncertain which direction it would come from. "It's been over eight months. What makes you think we need her, or even care if she lives or dies? She *abandoned* us."

"Don't care? Hmm," I huffed, resting the stick against the side of the table. "Then it wouldn't matter to you to know that she didn't abandon you at all. Her memory was erased, unbeknownst to her. She can't recall the final season of *Sons of Anarchy*, let alone her own fated destiny."

"How do you know this?" the chalky-eyed demon ventured, trepidation cracking his bruiser front.

"As luck and circumstance would have it, my horned and misshapen friend, I know *exactly* where she is. And right now, I can tell you, she is in very real danger."

Chairs slid from tables, screeching over cheap linoleum. Every demon present rose to their feet.

Kat positioned herself at their helm. She lorded over them in a wide-legged stance with her hands on her hips. "You will take us to her, *now*!"

"Oh, absolutely! The girl has no memories of anything otherworldly. By all means, let's take a bus of us, with all our ghoulish attributes," my fingers danced through the air, gesturing to the most off-putting amongst the crowd, "and pop by for a visit. That wouldn't be jarring at *all*."

"You cannot keep our leader from us!" Chalky-eyes barked, stamping his foot against the ground hard enough to make the floor shudder.

"Ah, ah, ah," I wagged my finger before me, "we don't get what we want when we throw a tantrum. And, I have no intention of keeping her from you. The moment she gets her memory back, I am sure she will gladly reassert herself as your valiant chieftess. In the meantime, if you care for her well-being, you will want to keep her safe and free from unnecessary emotional scarring, just as I do."

Uneasy glances were exchanged around the room.

Wetting her onyx-painted lips, Kat stepped forward as the voice of her people. Flipping her hair over her shoulder, her chin lifted with determination. "What danger is she facing?"

"A Hellhound is loose somewhere on the Rhodes College campus." Pacing the length of the room, I purposely ignored their chorus of shocked gasps. "That's where your darling leader is living out her mundane life, for those of you not yet following along. She doesn't remember her powers, has no battle skills to fall back on. Meaning, if that ghastly mongrel stalks across her path, she has no way to defend herself. That's where all of you come in."

Chalky anxiously shifted, his breath quickening in anticipation. "We need to hunt the Hellhound."

Spinning, I threw my arms out wide. "Ding, ding, ding! Give that boy the solid gold Kewpie Doll! You want your leader back, safe and sound? Hunt. Seek. *Kill*."

"Hunt. Seek. Kill." Quiet at first, demonic voices joined together again and again. Each chant building and brewing into a pulsating call to war. *"Hunt. Seek. Kill!"*

Slowly, a smile snaked across my lips. Just like that, I had my army. All thanks to a little Conduit name dropping.

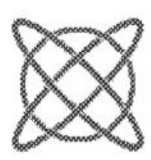

I don't normally struggle with low self-esteem. I'm a dashing swashbuckler with mind-control powers. As far as appeal to the fairer sex, I'm never left wanting. That said, I was feeling pretty damned good. Even had myself a cocky little strut going on. I played the hero and saved the princess. A platoon of demons were currently scouring the area for signs of the Hellhound, all whilst maintaining a safe distance from our damsel in distress. Sure, said damsel had no idea she was, or ever had been, in distress, but I still had every intention of cashing in on my white-hat reward.

Hmmm ... I might even do the little trick she likes that always makes her erupt in a high-pitched giggle I adore, I mused, and rapped on the door of her dorm room.

Hand curled around the edge of the door, Celeste eased it open. The apologetic expression she wore held the same potency of an icy shower. No, there would be no celebratory nookie. Not this night.

"Slight change of plans." Sucking air through her teeth, she pushed the door the rest of the way opened.

My shoulders deflated in blue-balled frustration. "It seems your room has come down with an infestation of Garretts."

The gang was all there. Celeste's slighty wacky Grams held up a miniscule *Juicy Couture* nightie, seemingly judging if she could wriggle into it.

Laughing, Celeste's younger sister Kendall shook her head, flaxen locks cascading across her shoulder blades. Extracting the garment from her grandmother's hand, the once winged beauty tossed it back into her overnight bag. Oblivious to their antics, big—and I mean downright massive—brother Gabe slumped down on Celeste's bed. The springs screeched at the sudden impact of his formidable weight. Alaina, his very pregnant wife and ex-spirit guide, absentmindedly rubbed her swollen mid-section with one hand while the other poked through a tote stuffed with extra pillows and blankets. One by one, they greeted me with waves and warm smiles. All except for Gabe, who began audibly snoring the second his head hit the pillow. A girl's family actually *liked* me. That was as awkward a fit as stumbling into a Catholic mass naked ... which I may have done once at the turn of the century after gorging myself on the sacrificial wine.

"They just showed up," Celeste mouthed the words, in barely more than a whisper. "Apparently, they are staying here tonight because Grams wants the full *college* experience. Somehow, she even got my RA to agree. I don't know how. I suspect dark, voodoo magic, or the promise of cookies."

"Where are we all going to sleep?" Alaina asked. Surveying the cramped quarters, her features pinched like she had tasted something sour. "These beds are really small. My mass could easily take up two of them."

"Terin's bed is free," Kendall chirped. Flopping down on the aforementioned bed, she folded her legs in front of her and situated her bag on her lap to continue riffling through it. "I don't think it's a coincidence that she decided to sleep at a friends the second she got a glimpse of Grams' shortie robe."

Celeste spun on her, nose crinkling in disgust. "The ... *ugh*! Why? *Why* would you bring the shortie robe? You shouldn't even *have* the shortie robe!"

"Because I'm a cougar on a college campus! *Raaawwwrr!*" Grams playfully growled, pawing at the air with fuchsia painted nails.

"Grams!" Alaina snapped her fingers in correction. "We had a deal! No growling outside of the zoo. You're going to confuse the baby!"

Turning to face me, Celeste rolled her eyes skyward with such flair, I feared they would never venture down again. "Yeah, *that's* why she shouldn't make that noise."

Ignoring the jab, Grams scooted around Alaina's girth and clacked across the floor on beaded wedge heels. "Rowan! With that smile I bet you've charmed many a girl into odd sleeping arrangements. Go knock on the door next door and see if we can borrow their room for the night. Maybe they can shack up with friends. Tell them we have a pregnant one here that snores like a hibernating bear with a deviated septum and need the space. Bat the baby blues if need be. Heck, even give their tushes a squeeze if it helps!"

"Grams!" Celeste's face morphed a brilliant flame red. "Stop telling my boyfriend to hit on other girls!"

"You don't live with pregnant Alaina." Puffing her cheeks, Grams expelled an exasperated breath through pursed lips. "It's for the greater good, believe me. Just look at your brother."

Groaning, Gabe rolled to face the wall.

"My snoring broke him," Alaina admitted sheepishly.

"I don't know what you're complaining for. Just do what I do!" Kendall suggested. Pulling earbuds from her bag, she plugged them into her phone and thumbed her playlist to life. Next came a fuzzy pair of earmuffs that situated into place. A hunting hat with earflaps topped off the sensory deprivation layering.

"Because that looks comfy," Celeste *tsk*ed.

"*What*?" Kendall yelled to hear herself over her muting muffs.

"I said, you look comfy!" Celeste shouted back with a wide smile and two enthusiastic thumbs up.

Merrily returning the gesture, Kendall pulled her stuffed zebra, Mr. Hoofington, from her bag and gave him a squeeze.

"So … the romantic evening is out?" I ventured, eyebrows raising.

"For so many reasons," Celeste sighed, slumping against the frame of the door. "But since you brought friends, too, it seems you already knew that."

"Since I what?" Following her gaze, I spun to find Kat and Chalky-eyes—Horitz, as I had since learned his real name—huddled together in the hallway behind me, staring at Celeste like they had just watched Beyoncé sashay into the room. "Excuse me for a minute." I offered my beloved a smile before crossing the space to intercept the demons' fangirl freak out.

"Oh, my countess! It's her!" Horitz squealed whilst doing frantic jazz-hands. "I didn't believe you, but I can *feel* her presence! It's *her*!"

"You have got to shut up!" I hissed through my teeth. Ushering them farther down the hall, I risked a glance back.

Celeste pulled her chin in to her chest, staring back at the strangers gaping at her with open unease. I offered her an oddly timed salute as a form of comfort. Don't judge me; I panicked.

"*What are you doing here*?" I hissed.

"You tore me from my pack leader, *pirate*." Horitz's attempt at a gravelly bellow lost intimidation points with his child-like voice.

"Your leader is going to think you are a creeper stalker if you don't *back off!* Do you want her to run away and vanish? Because that's all that comes from the clingy vibe."

"No," Horitz whined. "We need her! She must stay with us. We will make her stay!"

Straightening my spine, I blinked at his theatrics. "And that's the stalker's motto. What I need from you is for you to reclaim at least an ounce of your cool right now. Kat, can you help rein him in?"

I glanced to the goth-beauty in search of her calm indifference.

The response I received was buckling knees and free flowing tears which streaked mascara down her face. *"I love her so much!* I … I feel whole when I'm near her! I haven't felt that in so long!"

Arms falling slack at my sides, judgment radiated from my stare. "Really, Kat? I expected more from you."

Tossing yet another forced smile over my shoulder, I scraped Kat off the ground and shoved them both farther down the hall with more force than necessary. Out of ear shot had become my crucial new objective.

"Did I fail to mention there's a Hellhound on the loose that you're supposed to be *hunting*? You two keep this up and you might as well light torches and lead them straight to our memory deficient Chosen One!" Snarling through my teeth, I contemplated knocking their heads together.

Horitz couldn't tear is dreamy-eyed gaze off Celeste, who turned away to help Alaina search for something. "We couldn't detect the beast. So, we thought we would follow you and let you know … and then, there she was."

"You looked for all of … what, five minutes?" I could feel the tendons bulging in my neck, yet couldn't seem to claim an ounce of chill.

"I love you!" Kat screamed to Celeste. Clamping her hand over her mouth, she looked as surprised at her outburst as the rest of us.

Horitz rose up on tiptoe, craning his neck one way then the other in search of a better view of everyone's favorite brunette. "There isn't a trace of the hound's scent anywhere within a five mile radius. Either it can take another form, has a killer cologne, or it's gone. Do you think if I asked, she would autograph my—"

I halted him with one finger. "Be it body part, or scrapbook, the answer is no. And since you two have proved yourselves *completely* worthless, I will handle this myself. Can I *at least* trust you to guard the perimeter of the building and make sure no ravenous beasts venture inside?"

They nodded a bit too enthusiastically.

"Without coming anywhere near her or freaking her out?"

That answer took a bit more contemplation, and matching looks of self-doubt. After a pause, they both bobbed their heads in agreement.

"Good. Go. Start now, while I clean up your mess, children." I motioned them away with a flick of my wrist. Then, stood firm with my eyebrows raised while they retreated like cast off mutts.

By the time I found my way back to Celeste, she was doing her best to stifle a laugh at our mess of a night. "New friends of yours? They seem ... neat."

"Yeah, they don't ... *people* well," I admitted, watching them vanish down the stairwell. "Unfortunately, they did remind me of something I have to take care of tonight. Can we raincheck our plans?"

"Our plans to stay in and watch *Magic Mike* with my Grams? I can't imagine why you would want to miss that!" she gasped, feigning shock. "You can raincheck that; *I* am fated to endure it."

Curling my hand around the back of her neck, I pulled her to me and dotted a kiss to the top of her head. "Tomorrow night, I'll make it up to you. Promise."

"Are you gonna show me your best Channing Tatum moves?" she asked, biting her lower lip.

"I'll make him look like a rhythmless cad." I winked.

Glancing into the room, I watched the other Garrett women settling in for their cinematic treat of man-meat.

"Do me a favor," I knew I needed to release my hold on her, yet couldn't quite bring myself to do it, "just ... promise me you'll stay in tonight."

"And risk missing out on a moment of this crazy party train?" Her lighthearted quip trailed off when she noticed my steely intensity. "I ... I'm not going anywhere. Promise."

With one final kiss lingering her taste on my lips, I ventured. The hero, hell-bent on saving his princess.

CHAPTER 4

Finding a vacant hallway, I *poofed* off in a wisp of smoke. My destination? The far reaches of the South Pacific. The good thing about mystical teleportation? Lightning fast travel time and never having to wrestle through airport security. The shit side of it? Never accruing any frequent flier miles. The demonic struggle is real.

Solidifying in a cave beneath the ocean's surface, I said a silent prayer of thanks for the convenient air pocket within the grotto and shook off a shiver of claustrophobia.

"This place smells like sea water and yesterday's catch of the day." I cringed, trying to distract myself from the weight of the ocean pressing down from above with nothing but a layer of rock to protect me.

"Rowan Wade," a husky voice growled.

I turned to find Malise, Queen of the Merpeople, soaking in a hot spring with her glistening silver tail flapping in the churning bubbles. Sentries perched on the rocky ledges on either side of her. The stoic men stood statue still, all bulging muscles and pointy sticks. Malise waved her hand in what I guessed to be a signal for them to unclench.

Head listing to the side, a lock of hair fell across my forehead and tangled in my lashes. "Malise, *always* a pleasure."

That wasn't a line. From the waist up, Malise was the loveliest specimen of the feminine form one could ever hope to lay eyes on. Wide turquoise eyes, hair a brilliant golden shade only found in the most dazzling of sunsets, and luscious breasts that would render the most skilled linguist into a babbling idiot. From the waist down, however, she was a fish. Sexually speaking, it was very confusing.

Rocking forward, she swam the length of the hot spring in two gentle splashes. Elbows on the edge of the rocky wall, Malise beckoned me closer with one curl of her finger.

Closing the distance between us, I crouched down with my forearms resting on the tops of my thighs. “Your Highness,” I stated with a respectful tip of my head and open leer.

Hoisting her upper body farther out of the water—which gave me a *bountiful* display of cleavage—she whispered in my ear, “Do you remember what I said I would do to you if I ever saw you again?”

Clearing my throat, I rocked back on my heels. Distance was imperative. “If memory serves, it involved slicing off my testicles and relocating them into my nostrils.”

Head tilted, she beamed up at me with a smile which could lure any sailor into her grasp. “And yet, here you are.”

“Please trust I am rather fond of that particular part of my anatomy and wouldn’t be here unless it was under the most *dire* of circumstances.”

Behind her, one of the guards snorted his amusement. Easy for him to scoff when it wasn’t his jewels in the vise.

Glancing over her shoulder, Malise exchanged cynical smiles with her protector. Begrudgingly, she turned her attention back to me. “Tell me, my salty sailor, what dire situation brought you here to beg for my help? Shall I assume it’s about a girl?”

Standing up, I shook out my cramping legs. “Why would you think that?”

"Maybe the firm set of your jaw and the protective flame burning behind your eyes?" One alabaster shoulder rose in a casual shrug. "Or, it's because your species is insanely predictable. With human males it is *always* about a girl."

Rubbing a hand over the back of my neck, my lips twisted to the side in a sardonic half-grin. "It could be said that the love of a woman can be traced to the root of all things good and evil. That said, I have a bigger, more foreboding problem brewing."

Malise held up one hand to inspect her dagger-like opalescent fingernails. "And what makes you think *I* can be of any help?"

"Merfolk have been around since the beginning of time in one form or another," I explained, shoving my hands in the pockets of my khaki slacks. "Your kind hovers beneath the surface watching what unfolds above with detached interest. Never intervening, no matter the situation."

Malise let her head fall back, considering me through narrowed eyes down the bridge of her nose. "This is bordering on offensive, *pirate*. Do you have a point?"

Rocking back on my heels, I fixed my sapphire stare on her. "You've seen it all: the good, the bad, and the unmentionable. And it's on the latter that I need your expertise—a sensitive topic even demons dare not speak of."

"I'm intrigued." Malise drummed the pads of two fingers against her bottom lip. "What could *possibly* make the bad boy of the Underworld nervous?"

"In a word?" I asked, hitching one brow. "Hellhounds."

The elegant queen's face fell, her complexion draining to seafoam white. "Those monstrosities? They're extinct, and even then their reign of terror was far too long."

In the distance I could hear the steady roar of rushing water, making my nerve endings twitch to teleport topside. "Pure bloods are long extinct, true enough. However, rumors of hybrids infected through a Hellhound virus aren't exactly a new development."

Slapping her hands onto the smooth cavern floor, Malise hoisted herself out of the water. Her tail flipped up, splattering fat droplets over the front of my shirt. Air moved, her fins shimmered, and a pair of long, delectable legs appeared.

My leer was halted by one raised finger.

"This friendship will only work if we have a no touching, no lingering gazes rule." Before I could contest that declaration, Malise pivoted to address her guards. "Leave us. I can surely handle one randy demon, or I'm not fit to be queen."

Dutiful nods, and both guards dove head first into the hot spring, which proved to be much deeper than it appeared. Malise watched their tails vanish, and every last ripple subside before dragging her stare back up to mine.

A thin layer of steely resolve could not mask the visible fear which bubbled beneath the surface and quaked through her tone. "Let me first say that if the Hellhound virus is active, you may want to set up permanent residence here, Mr. Wade. No place on earth will be safer. Those infected will have the same appetite for pain and violence as the original beasts, without the element of control. They will go for the anguish—making their victim writhe in agony before extracting their soul."

"And each victim gets marked with the brand of the beast in the process," I filled in, a knot of dread tightening in my gut.

Malise dibbed her head in regal confirmation. "If—by some slim chance—the hound fails to kill those bearing the mark, the infection will spread to them. In that case, expect an outbreak. Odd thing about this illness?" Leaning in, she dropped her voice to a conspiratorial whisper, "Humans are the more volatile ones when infected. Demons experience a bit more … poetic control. They still kill, but with a more colorful flair. Something about those ailments combined creates a maniacally plotting rogue that makes Jack the Ripper seem like a nursery maid."

"There has only been one victim so far. There isn't enough evidence to pose any kind of guess if a human or demon is behind it. That bears the question …" I trailed off, unease catching the words in my throat.

"Question?" Malise prompted.

Clenching my teeth to the point of pain, I stared down at the damp rocks beneath my boots. "Have Hellhounds ever been known to target a particular family or person?"

"Like a Great White tormenting a family off the coast of Cape Cod?" She chuckled. Flipping her legs over the edge of the hot spring, Malise slid back into the water with barely a splash. The water flashed silver with the return of her scales. "I suppose any creature could become fixated on a particular being or bloodline if so provoked. If you find that to be the case, you need to fill in the unfortunate target with the knowledge of what's coming for them and convince them to run like hell. Once a Hellhound locks on a victim, it's only a matter of time until they get what they are after. The beast will bat them around in a vicious game of cat and mouse before devouring them. In the end there will be nothing left. That treasured piece of us that moves on into the hereafter will be reduced to nothing more than a dog treat."

Vehemently, I shook my head. "There has to be another way. Sh—*They*," wincing at my mistake, I quickly corrected it, "can't know about this."

A knowing smile brightened Malise's face with the brilliance of the first light of dawn.

"Ah, so it *is* about a girl. A pirate in love, sounds like a romance novel in the making." Falling into a backstroke, she flutter kicked to the opposite side of the hot spring. "If you want to save your bonnie lass, your only option is to find the infected Hellhound, whoever or whatever it is, and kill them before the virus can spread like the toxin it is."

An image of Celeste flashed behind my eyes. A memory of her surrounded by flames, her body battered and beaten, as she faced off against the Countess. She was a true warrior, a beacon for good in the swelling sea of darkness.

"She wouldn't want me to hurt anyone." I loathed to admit.

Bobbing upright, Malise fixed me with an icy stare. "Then you've already lost her. Don't deny who you are, Rowan. The blood of innocents has *already* stained your hands. At least *this* time you'll have noble intent behind it. Find the beast. Protect your girl. And *don't* call on me again."

With those as her parting words, the queen arced out of the water and plunged to the depths with swan-like elegance.

Still reeling from Malise's declaration, I reclaimed the classification of corporeal in a utility closet down the hall from Celeste's dorm room. Running my fingers through my hair, I puffed my cheeks and longed for the days when I could take troubling matters of the paranormal nature to the Chosen One and her band of do-gooders. They would have found a way to humanely dispose of the homicidal canine before nightfall. Left to my own devices, I saw no choice but to check in and make sure Celeste hadn't been made into kibble *or* bits, then hit the streets and *hope* I stumbled onto a soul-munching monster pooch.

It wasn't the most efficient plan, but was the best I could come up with stone sober.

Opening the closet door, I poked my head out. After a quick glance in either direction, I stepped out and immediately slammed into two co-eds exiting the showers.

"Mid-terms be damned, we *have* to go to O'Malley's tonight!"

"Uh, yeah! How can my future honey finally see me and start falling love with me if I'm not at *every* show? *Oof*!"

Their girlish rambling cut off at the moment of our awkward impact—for good reason. Their lack of apparel made the collision downright intimate. The more petite of the two was clad only in a towel. Her curvaceous friend wore what *would* have qualified as a bath robe, if it was three inches longer and considerably less see-through. Side-note: her nipple to breast ratio tipped significantly in favor of the later.

Wet hair clinging to their shoulders, they both glanced from the closet, to me, and back again with furrowed brows. At a loss for a plausible excuse, I opted for the obvious. Swaying on my feet, I raised my eyebrows and pantomimed struggling to focus.

"Thought that was the bathroom," I whispered a few octaves too loud. "I wouldn't go in there if I were you."

"*Tsk-uh*." Towel-girl cringed her disgust and twitched her way past me.

"Pity, he's hot." Following her friend, the other lass's leer wandered straight to third base as she passed.

"I'll remember you fondly and think of you often!" I called after them.

Turning on my heel with an amused smirk, I strode the remaining distance to Celeste's door.

Hand raised, I rapped softly with two knuckles.

Through the door came a shrill shout. "How *dare* you use a Draw Four on me! I am carrying your child! *What kind of monster are you?*"

The door swung the open. Celeste wore the impassive expression of someone struggling *not* to go on a rampage. Behind her, Alaina heaved herself off the ground and stomped into the bathroom, slamming the door behind her.

"I'm the worst kind of monster." Tossing his cards down on the floor, Gabe slouched back against the bed. "The kind that got married, impregnated my wife, and learned life is bigger than my own stupid emotions. You might want to look into that last part."

"*Are you insane?*" Grams hissed through her teeth, scrambling off the floor. "You can't say that to a pregnant woman! If I don't go pry her out of the bathroom now, she'll roost there!"

Kendall seconded the sentiment by swatting at her brother.

Slowly, Celeste wet her lips. "So, how's *your* night going?"

Sucking air through my teeth, I tried to think of an acceptable lie that would make her hate me an iota less. Short of claiming I stormed into a burning building to save a family of kittens, I had nothing. "Not much better," I began, shoving my hands in my pockets. "I didn't get done what I needed to. I'm going to have to—"

"If you say you're leaving again, I'm going with you." Crossing her arms over her chest, her tone left no room for argument or discussion.

"I don't know if ..." I trailed off as the bathroom door opened once more.

With an arm around her shoulders, Grams ushered Alaina back into the room.

"Look who's baaaack!" Grams announced with a singsong chirp.

"Gabe," Alaina sniffled, "Grams pointed out to me that my outburst *may* have been my emotions talking. And that, I apologize for. Then, she went on to tell me that if I didn't do Kegel exercises, after the baby comes I will pee on myself a little every time I sneeze. That made me cry for a whole new reason."

"I either come with you or will be sentenced to talking about the strength of my uterine wall with my *grandmother*." Celeste glared daggers at me, daring me to argue. "What's it going to be, Rowan? Keep in mind there *is* a wrong answer here, one that you will be punished mercilessly for."

"Well," I shrugged, mouth curling into a smirk, "the uterine wall thing could benefit me—"

"Finish that sentence and we're breaking up."

"Don't you start the next hand without me!" Kendall giggled. In slipper-clad feet, she stepped over the Uno game and made the three strides to us. All traces of her smile vanished the second she edged up beside her sister. "For the love of all that is good and pure, take me with you."

"What makes you think we're going anywhere?" Celeste asked, her voice betraying her by raising a guilty octave. The lass had many talents, being an effective liar wasn't one of them.

Kendall ticked the evidence off on her fingers. "You haven't committed to the evening by taking your shoes off since Rowan left the first time. You've checked your phone no less than five times a minute—which seems excessive even to *me*, and my phone is my life. And the second he knocked, you rocketed off the floor at a speed that defied all laws of physics and gravity. Look, if you two wanna go cozy up somewhere and get freaky, that's all you. No judgments here. I just beg you to have mercy and drop me off at the nearest coffee shop with Wi-Fi first. I am willing to negotiate terms to make this happen. What's it gonna take? Do your laundry for a month?"

Celeste's almond-shaped eyes narrowed. I could almost hear her mind ticking in search of the perfect bargaining chip. "That, and over Christmas break you have to be the one to go down into Gram's creepy-ass basement to bring up all the decorations."

Kendall's face crumbled with a blend of terror and revulsion. "Even those little elf statues with the pointy hats? Those things creep me out."

"Even the elves."

"Fine," Kendall relented, and offered her sister her hand. The two shook on it, then turned to me with matching expectant stares.

"So, where are we going?" they chorused in perfect Garrett unison.

"Really, I hadn't planned—"

"You're going?" Alaina inquired, interrupting my protest to the contrary. A bit of her former eagle essence showed through in the avian twitch of her head. "Where to?"

"*Is it a club*?" Grams perked up, her drawn on eyebrows rocketing into her hairline. "I've been practicing twerking, and I want to try it out on some hotties!"

Every soul in the room recoiled as Grams' joints creaked into prime twerking position.

"You can't go!" Alaina whined, rubbing her belly. "You have to teach me those exercises! You can't make a pants wetting claim like that and then just leave. That's cruel!"

Tangerine glossed lips sagging into a deep frown of defeat, Grams righted her posture. "You're right. I'll stay in with you tonight. But tomorrow? I'm gonna twerk enough to make Miley blush!"

Flopping down on the bed beside her husband, Alaina gave Gabe's shoulder a gentle shove. "I'm sorry the nasty pregnancy monster reared its ugly head again. Why don't you go out with them, sweets? Have some fun!"

Gabe's head lolled in her direction, his long legs stretched out and crossed at the ankles. "Because I look like I'm up for a party? Babe, I'm just waiting for a long enough lull in the conversation for it to be considered acceptable for me to start snoring and drooling on myself again."

Leaning into him, Alaina rested her chin on his shoulder. "You work so hard and take such good care of me. Plus, fun nights out are going to be in short supply once the baby comes. Then our time will be filled with midnight feedings and diaper explosions."

"What's a diaper explosion?" Keni whispered to her sister.

"Picture a piñata full of your favorite things," Celeste explained. "It's the exact *opposite* of that in the worst way imaginable."

"I'm past the point of needing crazy nights out." Reaching around her head, Gabe lovingly combed his fingers through his bride's hair. "I have proudly entered the phase where 'Netflix and chill' means exactly that, and it sounds like a heavenly evening."

"Ugh!" Sitting up, Alaina shoved his shoulder. Gabe, the fortress of testosterone he was, didn't budge. "If you acted any more like a grumpy old man, you'd be on Grams' front porch yelling at neighbor kids to stay off the grass."

"They leave divots!" he countered.

"Okay, now *I'm* insisting you go." Grams scowled, swatting him off the bed.

Grumbling, Gabe obliged.

"Fine," he begrudgingly relented. "Where exactly is the night taking us?"

All eyes turned to me, a mild inconvenience since my mind had suddenly gone blank. I needed to find a Hellbeast, not a new favorite lager! Still, the right destination *could* help distract them enough for me to continue my search. "Uh ... I heard the band at a pub called O'Malley's is killer."

CHAPTER 5

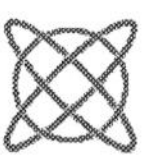

Karma was a sadistic strumpet that thoroughly enjoyed socking me in 1e danglers when I least expected it. Running my tongue over my top teeth, I 1arveled at how lackadaisical I had become that I hadn't seen this coming. Or, ɔ be more accurate, I hadn't seen *him* coming.

Caleb.

On stage at O'Malley's he strummed his guitar and caterwauled into the ıic, much to the crowd's delight.

When we were thrust into this new life a few months ago, I took ainstaking measures to keep Celeste and myself away from the raven-haired ain in my ass. I memorized his schedule and routine, and whenever the need rose, I would usher my trusting lass along paths that would purposely avoid ıy accidental meetings. With time, I grew a little lazy. On more than one ccasion, we would be lounging somewhere on campus and that infuriating ishman would stroll right past. Never once did he look her way. Never once did 1e bat an eye in his direction. It seemed in this alternate reality the two were visible to each other. Taking comfort in that, I settled in to an existence issfully, euphorically Caleb-free.

Until that moment.

There was no avoiding him. Screaming Irish rock into the mic with a gor that made the veins along his neck bulge, every lass on the dance floor reeched and whistled their appreciation of his efforts. Hair clung to his sweat-reaked forehead. The black T-shirt he wore was practically soaked straight through. Thralls of females swarmed the stage, each dancing a little raunchier than the next in hopes the green-eyed crowd-pleaser would notice them.

Beside me, Celeste sipped her beer and gazed his way over the frothy rim.

"This place is loud," I shouted over the music. "Doesn't it seem a bit loud? I don't know about the rest of you, but a quiet coffee shop would be bliss about now."

"Oh!" Kendall spun on her barstool, swatting at the air with frantic jazz-hands. If she heard me, her own enthusiasm trumped my suggestion. "I forgot to tell you! I auditioned for *Peter Pan*, and I was offered the part of Peter Which is amazing, but they want to put me in a harness and *fly me* around the room. That's terrifying! You know I don't like heights. Maybe I could ask the director to consider me for Wendy instead? Or Tinkerbell … no, she would probably have to fly, too. Does it make me sound like too much of a diva actress if I ask to be recast?"

"Yes, absolutely," Celeste mumbled, her stare not wavering from Caleb If her indifferent tone was any indication, she hadn't heard one word her siste said.

A chestnut-haired lad swaggered up to Kendall, flipping his hair from hi smoldering eyes.

Gabe halted him with one threatening hand slapped to the kid's narrov chest. Even perched on his barstool the beastly Garrett was eye to eye with th would-be suitor.

"Notice the bracelet, Abercrombie," he growled, jerking his chin in th direction of Kendall's accessory. "She's *underage*. Seventeen, to be exact. Kee walking."

Lover boy altered his course without breaking stride. Wise choice.

Oblivious to all of this, Kendall sagged in defeat.

"I don't want to offend the director. I guess I have to ... *fly*," she gulped.

"That'll be great," Celeste half-heartedly agreed. No, not even half her heart. Maybe like a tenth of it.

"I didn't fancy you a fan of Celtic punk," I muttered against her ear, my hand brushing the small of her back.

Spinning to face me, guilt white-washed her face. "What? Who? Him? No!"

"That was a very convincing long-winded ramble. Did you practice that for maximum eloquence?" Dropping my chin, I grinned up at her from under my brow.

Tucking her hair behind her ear, she shrugged off my claim.

"Sure, he's hot in an *obvious* kind of way, but you're more ..." The ever witty Conduit trailed off, her eyes widening as if every possible adjective she had even known suddenly leaked out her ear.

Eyebrows raised, I rolled my head in a half-circle in hopes it would spur along the much anticipated end of her sentence. "The longer this hesitation drags on the more insulting it becomes."

Her delectable lips twisted into the *you're an idiot* smirk she frequently ast my way. Sliding from her seat, she hooked her index finger into my belt oop and tugged me body-skimming close. Tipping her face to mine, she gazed p at me with an open acceptance that took my breath away. "Closing in on a ear together, and he still gets jealous. I kinda love that."

"You're trying to distract me from your *very* effective feminine wiles, ut still have to deny the appeal of the Irish stallion," I murmured against her ps, bathing in the hypnotic pull of her tender touch.

"He's not the only hot guy here," she stated in place of an answer. "Do ou have any idea how many girls have checked you out since we walked in? nough to give the sweaty guitar hero a run for his money. Each lovely lady that leered your way has taken one look at me and wondered how on earth we ended up together."

"Because—" My protest was silenced by the tips of her fingers pressing to my lips.

"I'm sorry, *insecure, crazy time* is over. Now we're heading back to reality. On the planet *I* live on—despite eye candy galore—your eyes haven't wandered once nor have you left my side."

The truth in that sentiment struck me with enough force to make my heart stutter in my chest. She was right. Other than keeping vigil for threatening Hellhounds, not once had I scanned the room for possible *talent*. Gun to my head, I couldn't describe one female in the room that *wasn't* my hoodie clad date with her messy bun, or her little sis. Admiring the female form was a favorite past time of mine, yet I hadn't even been tempted. Why?

The answer shuddered through me.

Because what started as a simple taste testing of a fantasy I thought could never claim, morphed into something far deeper. All I could ever want, or need, lived within the little brunette morsel before me.

"Hot is easy to achieve," Celeste continued, clueless to my life changing insight. "Sexy is a matter of opinion. You're something far better. You're … *mine*."

Rising on tiptoe, she brushed her lips to mine.

Heart hammering in my chest, I realized the magnitude of my crushing need for her.

"I …" The words couldn't form in my Mohave parched mouth.

At a loss for usual linguistic talents, I pressed my forehead to hers.

With the side of one knuckle, Celeste traced my jawline. "There's word people use in moments like this. It starts with an L and ends with—"

“Bitter resentment,” I finished for her. “It’s a completely inadequate word.”

“Hmm,” she murmured, the tip of her nose brushing mine in an intimate caress. “Sounds like a cursed word. We should find another.”

Catching her face in the cradle of my hands, I lifted her gaze to mine. “How about, you’re my habit … my addiction I’d sooner die than quit.”

Our lips met with fevered urgency. Weaving my fingers into her hair, I pulled her to me, molding her body to mine. Was it my imagination, wishful hinking, or could I *feel* the heat from Caleb’s emerald gaze burning into me?

Let the sodding Irishman watch.

Whatever happened before, whatever got us where we were, she was *mine* now. I celebrated that victory by tracing my hands down her spine and nibbling on her lower lip in a way that earned a throaty moan from *mo chroi*.

“Ugh,” Kendall groaned, pantomiming a dry heave. “Gabe, our sister’s voyeuristic tendencies are making me heave. You may need to take me home.”

“That’s probably for the best.” Sliding from his barstool, Gabe rose to ull, menacing height. “Otherwise I’m gonna kill the next douche bag that comes niffing around you, and drape him over my shoulders as a warning to all the thers.”

“Dude, that was dark.” Keni cringed, lacing the strap of her cross-body ag around her neck. “You need a nap … or a hug.”

Grunting his agreement, Gabe snatched his Carhart jacket off the stool eside him and stalked toward the door.

“As for you two,” Kendall warned, her eyes twinkling mischievously, ’m going to tell you the same thing I told Grams the night of the Senior Center uau: you’re still in public and *have* to keep your clothes on.”

Snorting at what I thought was a joke, I glanced down in time to see eleste’s face fall into a frown. “Yeah, that was a *looooong* night.”

The youngest Garrett gave her sis a shoulder bump of solidarity. “You might want to think about taking off, too. The next act is warming up, and their vibe is very hipster meets glee club. Nothing but mash-ups of eighties rock and indie albums will follow.”

While the two said their abbreviated good-byes, my gaze wandered to the upcoming band.

“Son of a …” I spat through my teeth. Diving into the grinding masses, tossed a quick, “Gotta hit the restroom,” over my shoulder.

Dodging and weaving through the crowd, instead of breaking right tc the bathrooms, I banked left toward the stage.

“Hey, Celeste, how about a fun night out?” Grumbling to myself, skirted around a randy couple with wandering hands and no inhabitations. “It’l be a scarring reunion with every demon you’ve ever met, and could potentiall ruin this peaceful little existence you’ve been enjoying by plunging yot headlong into a world of war and chaos. But, hey, we had a good run, right?”

“What?” a buxom blonde asked as I bumped past her.

“Not you, miss. Nice use of fish-net, by the way.”

Shrugging off my random rant, she went back to shimmying her fu bags.

Breaking through the sweat swarm, I grabbed the scrawny fella pullin his guitar from its case by the shoulder and forced him to face me. “Hi, pal, it’ been a while.”

Any questions I may have had about Eddie remembering me wer answered by his eyes bulging to goose eggs.

“Wha … *hi*?” he stammered.

Behind him, his three cohorts snapped to attention. I never took th time to learn the names of the members of the Dark Army Glee Club. They wer lackeys, why bother? It had been easier to adopt Celeste’s monikers for then

Red, Lone Twin—his brother had been lost in the battle at Gainesboro—Boil Face, and ...

"Eddie, it's been a long time." Pulling the Eddie Munster look-alike in right to my side, I prevented the fidgety little twerp from bolting. "How ya been?"

The portion of Eddie's face that *wasn't* covered by a big, bushy beard visibly blanched. Letting his hair grow out and sweeping it to the side masked his extreme widow's peak. Further distraction came from his revealing skinny jeans and James Dean T-shirt—which he wore ironically, of course.

"I ... *uh* ... think you have me confused with someone else," he tammered.

"Oh yeah?" I pondered, squeezing his shoulder hard enough to make him whimper. "Let's get acquainted then. What's your name?"

"Ed-Edward," he squawked, swallowing hard.

"A whole new start, and that's the best you could come up with? rilliant." Shaking my head at his vast nincompoopary, I spun him to face me. Now for the bonus round; who am *I*?"

Eddie's mouth opened and shut like a swinging screen door. Nothing seeped out except a high-pitched squeak. In my peripheral vision I caught sight f his friends shaking their heads and making slicing motions across their hroats.

"If I were you, I wouldn't steal answers from your friends." Sucking air hrough my teeth, I faked concern. "They might not have your best interests at eart."

"Rowan! Your name is Rowan Wade!" Eddie exclaimed in one long-winded ramble.

“Dude, that was *totally* an Eddie move,” crossing his arms over his chest, the demon formerly known as Boil Face scoffed. “Edward would *never* have wussed out like that.”

My mouth opened to argue in favor of Eddie’s wise act of self-preservation when Boil Face’s updated appearance gave me pause. The long, scraggly beard he’d grown covered more than half his demonic skin condition. Wide, cat-framed glasses took up another quarter. Add to that his knit beanie cap, neatly buttoned flannel shirt, and crocheted infinity scarf, and he was *actually* passable as human.

Wagging a finger at him, I then pressed it to my lips in contemplation. “This is a good look for you. It makes me want to spoon out my own eyes marginally less.”

“That’s really all anyone can hope for.” Boil Face, hence-forth known as Beard Face, chuckled and let one shoulder rise and fall in a nonchalant shrug.

“The question remains,” gripping Eddie’s collar, I held him where he was, “the Counsel did a big ole memory wipe. Yet, here I find you, memories intact and swarming Caleb. You boys wouldn’t be trying to awaken his inner Titon would you?”

“Not at all!” Eddie squirmed for his freedom, but gained no ground. Adorable little troll. “As far as we can tell, we didn’t matter enough for the memory wipe. We’re like the R2-D2 of this saga.”

“We ran into Caleb a while back and he didn’t immediately pummel us which was a nice change of pace,” Lone Twin explained, straightening his bowtie and smoothing his blue blazer. “It didn’t take long to figure out he didn’t remember us. In fact, he thought we were kinda … cool. He even asked us to hang and got us a gig performing here three nights a week.”

“Plus,” Red, dubbed that for his fiery strands, added, “this hipster thing is really working for us!”

Lips pressed into a thin white line, I nodded. "Yes, I'm certain it's the ipster thing and not you hanging around with the likes of Caleb that has upped our social standing. What, do you scoop up his broken-hearted cast-offs?"

"I wish!" Eddie snorted, stumbling to regain his footing after I finally eleased my hold. "There *are* none."

Pulling back, I stared up at my former bloke with a newfound ppreciation. "*None!* Blimey! The lad's a machine!"

"No," Lone Twin corrected with a laugh, "there are no heartbroken cast-ffs. He tells all the girls up front that he's done with casual encounters and 'ants the real thing or nothing—which sounds *way* cooler with his accent. nyway, they all love him for it and hang around hoping for the chance to be his *eal thing*."

Silently fuming, my teeth ground to the point of pain. Call me selfish, ut I would much rather learn that Cal was getting an entire fleet's worth of im than to hear the brooding Irishman was pining for his one true love. specially since her taste still lingered on *my* lips.

Rubbing a hand over the back of my neck, I feigned indifference. "As appy as I am for Caleb and his steadfast resolve, they aren't my primary oncern at the moment."

"Whatever your drama is, why should we care?" Red snarled, puffed up n his own measly bravado.

Taking my time, I fixed my icy stare on each of them, dragging it slowly om one to the next. "In a word? *Hellhound*."

For a beat, none of them spoke.

Not one expelled the breath lodged in their throats.

They simply stared, blinking in disbelief.

It was Lone Twin that shattered the hush by spinning on Beard Face. *'hey aren't real! You swore they weren't real!"*

Pursing his lips, Beard Face scowled in my direction. "Fantastic. Now I'll never get him to sleep tonight."

Swinging my arms out wide, I clapped my hands in front of me. "Sorry about that, but at least I know all of you understand the severity of the situation. That'll be a fantastic time saver."

Gnawing on his lower lip, the twin's nervous gaze lobbed from me to the door and back again. "I'm actually frozen in fear. I didn't know that was a real thing. But here I am, rooted to this spot while my body tries to decide if I'm going to bolt for the door or evacuate my bowels right here."

Without a word, I took a precautionary step back.

In a sudden rush of panic Eddie seized the sleeve of my shirt in a white knuckled grasp. "Do you know this for a fact?" he gasped. "That there is *actually* a Hellhound prowling around? Do you have any idea what a claim like that *means*? For starters, we are in the exact *worst place possible*. Hellhounds love crowds! We might as well be standing at the door ringing the dinner bell. And let me tell ya, pal, if one bursts in here *none* of us would make it out alive!"

Wrapping my hands over his closed fists, I eased them from the now rumpled fabric. "I'm going to need you to breathe, and never, *ever* grab me like that again."

Glancing toward the bar, I found Celeste tipping a fresh long-neck to her lips. Brow furrowed, she watched our little spectacle with growing interest. Offering her a forced smile, I held up one finger to let her know I would be right there.

"That *is* the Conduit!" Beard Face stabbed one hand in the air in recognition, then let it fall to his side with a slap. "I thought so, but it was hard to tell without her scowling and threatening us."

"Correct me if I'm wrong," Red stuffed his hands in his pockets, his shoulders hunching inward, "but if there's a nasty monster on the loose, isn she *exactly* the person we want the hound to run into it? I mean, she's got that nifty super strength—even if she doesn't know it. In this type of situation she seems the girl to hide behind."

"No!" I snapped more harshly than I intended. "We handle this alone. None of this gets anywhere near Celeste."

"But we need to make it *our* problem?" Red pulled back as if questioning my sanity. "Why would *we* stick around at all instead of running to the farthest reaches of the planet without looking back?"

"I do like the sound of that option." Eddie pointed at Red and nodded his agreement.

Frustration bubbled through my veins, churning and writhing into a steady boil. Raising my hands in front of me, I curled them into tight fists. My thread of self-control hovered a strand from snapping.

"Normally, this is where I would threaten violence with the disclaimer that I don't have to lift a finger for all holy hell to be unleashed," I stated in an eerily calm tone, each word measured and clipped. "I would adopt my most villainous leer and remind you that at my whim I can turn you on each other in a blood bath of epic proportions. Lucky for you, I'm not that guy anymore."

Shooting a smug glance to his fellow glee clubbers, Red's paper-thin lips screwed to the side. "No, *you're* the guy that took advantage of a situation by swooping in and stealing his buddy's girlfriend the first chance you got. Now you live in constant fear that one day she'll snap out of this little spell and hand you your ass … after she kicks it up and down the length of the campus a few times."

The others had the good sense not to laugh. They each made the wise decision to shift uncomfortably and look anywhere but at us.

One hand falling to my side, the other ran over the stubble of my chin. To stifle the simmering rage clouding my vision, I took a mental five count. Stepping in close enough to chest bump the musically inclined demon, I shrank him under the weight of my stare. "Maybe I have selfish motives. I won't deny that. But who here doesn't? You've all admitted to liking these little lives you've carved out for yourselves. Well—*newsflash, ginger*—if Celeste comes in contact with that Hellhound, her memory could come rushing back. If that happens, all of *this*," I flicked a finger at their hipster get-ups, "goes away. No longer will you be able to pass as tortured artists that sorority girls shag because it's easier than *actually* becoming cultured themselves. Demons and beasties of all walks of life will flock here intent on killing *her* and becoming the new big bad in the demonic hierarchy. We will be thrust right back into a war with our only options being to fight, or retreat back to the Underworld."

Lone Twin squelched a whimper behind his fist. "I hate the Underworld It smells like feet and stale Fritos, and there's no Wi-Fi!"

His cocky façade faltering, a tremor of nerves quaked through Red' tone. "Don't you understand? What's coming ... it's the thing the darkness fears and it will *kill us all*."

"It's that bad, and worse," I admitted. "Even so, there's no outrunning it. If this beast decides to make itself some pups, it'll start a plague that wi swallow the world whole. The only options left are to lay down and die, jocke for position as a minion—*again*—or take a chance and help me protect what' turned out to be a pretty damned sweet existence. What do you say? Wanna tr on the symbolic white hero hat and see how it fits?"

Red shifted his gaze to his friends. One by one they set their bushy bearded jaws and nodded.

Squaring his bony shoulders, he ventured, "What do we need to do?"

"I promise not to make you handle any of the scary monster parts," clarified, stepping back to a less threatening distance. "All you have to do is hel me find the sodding thing. Then, you can hang out at a safe distance, pop som popcorn, and watch me kill it—or vice versa if I'm having an off day. Either way should be a great show. So, how about it? Shall we pat each other's bums and declare us a team?"

Before any of them could respond, I felt a fluttering tap on my upper arm. Turning, I fell into the warm molasses pools of Celeste's concerned gaze.

"Everything okay?" she asked, glancing from the Glee Clubbers to me and back again.

Unsure of that answer myself, I followed her gaze to my new potential mates with my eyebrows raised in expectant arches. "The lady asks an intriguing question."

A silent beat, then ...

"Absolutely." Red walked to meet Celeste, hand outstretched. "Hi, I don't believe we've had the pleasure. We're friends of Rowan's. We were just discussing a ... *uh* ... history project we're teaming up on."

"Rowan actually caring about his classes?" Celeste marveled, glancing at me as if I had suddenly sprouted a unicorn horn. One pace forward and she accepted Red's offered hand. "You all may be wizards to make such a wonder transpire, but I'm okay with it. I'm his girlfriend, Celeste, and *you* are my new best frien—"

The words lodged in her throat, pinned there by a pair of scuffed motorcycle boots clomping down the narrow stage stairs.

"Pardon me, brothas," Caleb drawled in his nonchalant brogue. "Oh, an' the lovely miss."

He pulled up short at the bottom of the stairs, as if slamming into an impervious wall the moment he saw *her*.

I watched their eyes meet for one agonizing beat. The primal sparks that flew between them clawed my heart from my chest and crushed it in the vicious talons of jealousy.

“Sorrah …” Dropping his chin, Caleb shook his head, as if to free himself of their magnetic pull, “I din’t mean tah interrupt.”

Celeste had yet to blink—or exhale.

“It’s … okay,” she mumbled, not in the breathless moan I feared but abject confusion. Her eyes narrowed, head tilting like she was trying to place him.

Her heart-shaped lips parted. I knew the line of questions forming there before she could utter a syllable. Go ahead and insert whatever vile and profane names for me that you will, because I did what I felt I had to do. Concentrating on the nearest blonde strumpet, I lured her to Cal like a Hizolovsk demon to tree sap. Whirling around, she twitched his way with the sashay of a cat in heat. Only then did I recognize her as the lass in the bathrobe I slammed into back at the dorms. In an odd way, I was proud to help bolster her dream of visiting his Emerald Isle.

“Caleb,” she purred with a seductive pout, lacing her arm with his, “you promised to teach me a couple cords on your guitar.”

“Aye, that I did.” A little encouragement from me and Caleb flung his arm around the lass and pulled her to him, much to her tittering delight. “No time like the present, yeah?”

One last mind bump, and I willed the pair toward the door and out of my hair. To my teeth-grinding, nostril-flaring regret, that infuriating mick fought against my influence.

Hesitating, he glanced back at Celeste as if the act alone pained him. “… hope tah see ya here again sometime.”

An aggravated *tsk* and the bathrobe beauty dragged him out the pub’s back exit.

The awkward moment that followed was shattered by Lone Twin's giddy giggle. "Oh, my gawwwsh, you guys! That was like a scene right out of *Pretty Little Liars*!"

CHAPTER 6

"Say it again."

"I love you, only you, and no one but you."

"Now, with a Jamaican accent."

"I love you, onlah you, an' no one but you."

"That was dreadful. It sounded like an Australian after extensive denta work."

"I don't know how else I can convince you!" Celeste laughed, bumpin my ribs with her elbow. Hand-in-hand we walked back to her dorm room "Seriously, I thought I knew the guy from somewhere. That is *all*."

"You know," I ventured, glancing her way out of the corner of my eye "nothing says I'm sorry like a little *Fifty Shades of Wade*."

Face falling blank, Celeste stared off in the distance. "What would tha freak show even *look* like?"

"A steel-boned corset and ass-less chaps. Oh, and you can wear costume, too."

Halting mid-step, her eyes crinkled at the corners. "I am both arouse and horrified by that mental image."

Turning on the ball of my foot, I tugged her to me. "It's the cheekbone and wavy hair. Much like Orlando Bloom, I could pass as a *stunning* woman."

Rising up on tiptoe, her lips teased over mine. "I'll take you just the wa you are … often and regularly."

My hand traced down the small of her back to the rise of one cheek. There, it lingered. “Can I request these *takings* be plentiful enough to require protein bars and Gatorade?”

“Play your cards right, sailor,” she murmured, nipping at my lower lip.

As a throaty growl tore from my throat, we were forced apart by a ampaging female, both of us stumbling back to regain our footing.

“*Ugh*. Friggin’ couples!” the perturbed lass grumbled, stomping between us in full huff. “Get a room! Or, in your case, a utility closet.”

“Friend of yours?” Celeste watched the girl shrink into the distance with bemused interest.

Brow pinched, and jaw slack, I finally placed the irritable vixen as athrobe girl’s bestie. “Groupie of that Celtic band. She’s cranky her mate won a rip to the back of the lead singer’s Shaggin’ Wagon and she didn’t.”

My gaze flicked to her face, searching for some flare of jealousy that nother woman *might* be in Caleb’s toned and rippling arms tonight.

Mouth curling into a downward C, her shoulders rose and fell in a oncommittal shrug. “She should probably thank her BFF. I’ve heard some of hose STD treatments are a real bitch.”

“Ah, to hear sonnets from your sharp tongue,” I wistfully mused.

Wearing the blissful blinders of contentment, we continued our stroll. er hand twined effortlessly with mine. The cool night breeze tossed our hair om our faces. Somewhere in the distance an owl hooted his greeting.

If life had taught me anything, it *should* have been that pure contentment could always be viewed as a warning—the ominous swell of music efore a brutal and merciless attack. Looking back, I realize my time with eleste softened me and muted the edges of my prickly memories. Turning the corner of the final bend that led to her residents’ hall, I peered down at her, wishing I could pause that moment and live in it forever. Had I listened, maybe I would have heard fate's conniving snicker at such a school boy fantasy.

Time slowed as my head turned.

A demonic shudder skittered down my spine, whispering of a nearing darkness.

Chest swelling protectively, I tightened my grip on Celeste's hand and pushed her behind me.

The body swung overhead, alabaster legs riding the night's gusts and thumping against the flagpole.

"*Rowan, what are you—*" Struck by a potent surge of my influence Celeste went limp. Catching her in the cradle of my arms, I swept her up before her skull could crack against the pavement.

Horitz appeared from nowhere; charging toward me, spikes sprouting across his heaving shoulders. His lips split into four quadrants and peeled back to reveal row after row of tiny, razor teeth. Black smoke churned into Kat' shape behind him. Joining his pursuit, a dagger slid from her wrist.

No time for the war the pair sought, I commandeered control of thei minds and ordered them to stop.

"How dare you harm our leader," Horitz snarled, spraying the sidewal with saliva. Thrashing against my hold, he gained no ground.

In lieu of explanation, I lolled their heads skyward and tensed at th masks of horror that stole over their features.

"You … found this?" The words trembled from Kat's lips, her shoulde deflating.

"The Conduit didn't see it." Forcing the words through clenched teett ragged breaths heaved from my chest. "I made sure of that. Get her back to he room and stay with her until I come for you."

Releasing my hold, I gave Horitz a moment to regain his footing and holster his demon attributes before easing Celeste into his bulging arms.

"It's horrifying." The mammoth fiend gaped up at the spectacle one final time as he accepted his savior into his loving embrace. "What shall I tell her family if they ask questions?"

"I don't care!" I snapped. *"Just keep her safe or what I will do to you will make this look like a mercy kill!"*

Kat placed a comforting hand on Horitz's rippling bicep. "We will die before we let anything happen to her," she assured me.

In a blink, the trio vanished.

Bile rising in my throat, I pivoted back to the gory display. It had been gift wrapped in painstaking detail. The bathrobed beauty I met that very night was secured to the flagpole right outside Celeste's building. Hands bound behind her and tied to her ankles made her back arch as if she were an enchanting mermaid whittled into the front of a ship. Moonlight glistened off the ruby gouges of her bountiful slashes and wounds. Empty eye sockets stared off into the oblivion. What was left of her skimpy dress flapped behind her like a sail. It was the mark on her mid-section that made this offering specifically for me. Carved into her gut—in deep, vengeful strokes—a skull and crossbones mocked my failure.

Fighting against tremors of rage, my first call was to the police.

My second, as sirens wailed in the distance, was to the Glee Clubbers.

Pulse pounding in my temples, I didn't know or care which of them answered the phone.

"Bearded Sex Symbols R Us, we hair because we care. How may I direct your call?"

"Find me Caleb," I growled. "Keep your distance, but *do not* lose sight of him. He's the Hellhound."

I clicked the line dead just as low beams of three cop cars illuminated the tragically macabre act. Craving violence, not conversation, I removed myself from the scene in a cloud of seething, billowing smoke.

CHAPTER 7

Swaying metal twanged beneath my pounding fist. From the other side of the door, a slide-lock hissed free. Rusted steel squealed at the rolling door eing forced across its aged track.

Beard Face greeted me with heavy, red-rimmed eyes. His button down hirt was half untucked, his hair stabbing from his head in greasy spikes, as if he ad just woke up. Urgency overpowering courtesy, I shoved my way into the hoebox-sized apartment that reeked of stale beer and ball sweat.

"Where is he? I trust the four of you treasured your limbs enough to ool what competence you have to find him." My lip curled from my teeth, very muscle in my body set on a hairpin trigger for violence.

Raking his fingers through his scraggly facial hair, Beard Face shook his ead. "Really, the threats aren't necessary."

I whirled on him in a blur of speed no human could muster. Seizing the abric of his shirt, I yanked him to me, nose-to-nose. "An innocent girl was torn part tonight. Her body strung up for all to see. *Caleb* walked out of the pub ith that very same girl. In my book, that makes threats *very* necessary."

"There was a time when you counted the lives of innocents as prizes." eard Face instantly cringed his regret for letting the words slip out.

Dropping my voice to a menacing whisper, I felt the deadly calm of ayhem snaking through my veins. "Can you imagine the power of a soul-ucking Hellhound *combined* with a Titon demon? Cal would become an nstoppable force of nature … *literally!* Our only advantage is that with the

Counsel's memory wipe he doesn't *know* he's a monstrous badass. We need to find him and put him down before he figures that out. Now, I will ask you one more time nicely, then I start texturizing that metal door with the back of your skull. *Where is Caleb*?"

"You lads know there's a whole world outside, yeah?" a familiar voice drawled from the next room. Rooted in that spot, I tipped my chin to my shoulder to listen. "With *real* people ya can talk to and *far* fresher air tak breath."

Wetting my lips, I blinked back the red haze tinging the edges of my vision. "Is he here?"

"Has been since we left the pub," Beard Face peeped.

Hands balled in tight fists, I spun on my heel. The only coherent though I could form was the deep desire to rip my once dear mate's head from hi shoulders. My hell-bent charge made it all of two strides. Snagged by the bac of my shirt, the ground was stolen from beneath me. Forehead bumping th ceiling, I kicked and flailed for my freedom. Rotating his wrist, my captor turne me to face him.

It seemed somewhere in my fury it slipped my mind that Beard Fac could go full Hulk.

The floorboards creaked beneath his sizeable mass. Formerly loose ski pulled taut over his colossal form. The button down shirt he wore hung fror him in shredded ribbons. Either merciful luck or unfortunate proportioning o his part kept his skinny jeans in place from the thighs up. As his facial feature swelled, his two eyes joined into one bowling ball sized optic nerve. Patientl he blinked my way and waited for me to stop kicking like a cartoon coyot falling off a cliff.

"If you're about done," Beard Face boomed, the vibration of his voic rattling my bones to the marrow. "Caleb *couldn't* have killed anyone. He walke that girl to her car, said goodnight, and came back in to watch our set. He left the pub with *us* and has been here since. *You've got the wrong guy.*"

Losing a bit of my vigor, my legs dangled loose beneath me.

"I'm gonna put you down. But, if you go on another rampage, I'll texturize the floor with your puny head. Got it?"

Nodding, my agreement knocked my male bravado down about six notches.

Slowly, the floor rose to meet me and the titanic cyclops granted me freedom.

Grinding the heels of my palms into my throbbing eyes, I rubbed my hands down my face and peeked around the corner that separated the Glee Club's foyer from the rest of their loft.

There he lounged, my would-be murderous monster, in a rickety folding chair adjusting the strings of his guitar. Concentrating on his task, the hair that fell across Cal's forehead hung there unchecked. My cursory sweep of the rest of the room found Red seated on the floor polishing off a pizza, while Eddie and one Twin submerged themselves in a video game world that transpired a long time ago in a galaxy far, far away.

Ducking back behind the dividing wall into the foyer—aka the roosting spot for their pungent foot wear—I pressed my fist to my lips. Even though Beard Face had returned to his more manageable size, he maintained a smug smirk of warning.

"All those times when Celeste was openly hostile with you guys, I thought she was overreacting," I muttered, my hand muffling my voice. "That despite her dating choices, she secretly harbored demonic prejudices. But ... now? Now I think she had the patience of a saint for not pounding each of you into the ground in her own private game of Whack-a-Mole. *That guy*," I stabbed an accusing finger toward Mr. Dreamy McDreamerson in the next room, "*was the last person to be seen with a girl that was killed in a horribly psychotic fashion.* Yet, here you all sit, doing God only knows what!"

"Please lower your voice. I don't want to go mongo again and sit on you, but I will. And," his bearded chin lifted in a haughty fashion, "if you must know, we were laying down some sick tracks."

The wheels of my mind whirred, spinning and clicking in search of some meaning to the gibberish he spouted. "Clarity in the form of non-nerd lingc would be appreciated."

"He was playing his guitar and we were recording it. He is a YouTube star and doesn't even know it," he giggled, his shoulders rising to his ears wit giddy excitement. "We use it to meet girls. So far it's been a huge bust, bu we're staying optimistic. Around Valentine's Day it could be a gold mine!"

Needing silence from his ramblings before I made him hulk out and bea himself to death, I held up one hand in warning. "I'm sorry I asked. I *really* am See, I don't care about your ploys or schemes to get a little touch fron *someone*. The only information I need from you—possibly ever again—is Caleb was out of your sight for even a minute tonight?"

A beat of silence.

Chewing on the inside of his cheek, Beard Face mulled over th question.

"I'll take that as a yes. *How long*?" I barked, taking a threatening ste forward.

"I don't know, we were setting up," he shot back, his size swelling jus enough to make me tip my head to maintain eye contact. "Twenty minute tops."

"It still could be done in that time, especially by supernatural means Even I heard the hint of doubt that tainted my once adamant argument.

As if cued by my uncertainty, Caleb's head peeked around the wall. Offering me a half-smile and nod of acknowledgement, his dimple the ladies swooned over made a brief cameo. "Ev'rything okay out here?"

In place of an answer, I suppressed the glower at Beard Face. "You want proof? Fine. Tomorrow night at the pub, *we* watch, *we* confirm, and *I* make *my* move."

"Sounds ominous," Caleb chuckled. Head listing to the side, he considered me. "Hey, din't I see you at the club tonight, brotha? You were there with a wee brunette. The two of you make a right handsome couple."

Reluctantly, I craned my neck his way and bristled at the blatant sincerity slathered across his features. "*You* … don't speak of her again, or I *will* rip your throat out." While his eyes widened in what I assumed to be insincere shock, I spun back on Beard Face. "Tomorrow, we get our proof."

Without another word, I disappeared from the flat of the desperate, lonely, and possibly possessed.

"What is he doing?" Caleb muttered to Eddie out of the corner of his mouth the next night at the pub.

Dragging his index finger over the rim of his margarita, Eddie popped his salt encrusted digit in his mouth. "He thinks you're evil."

Sitting directly beside Cal, I leaned in with one elbow on the table and glared his way with pressure-cooker intensity. "I know you, Caleb—"

"Even though we've only met twice." Cal nodded, and tipped a long neck to this lips.

"Watching you across the room wouldn't work," I continued, whilst ignoring all boundaries of personal space. "You're too shifty for that. So, I will be right here. Watching ..."

"A complete strang'r," Caleb filled in, rolling his beer bottle between his palms, "as we all are at some point in the day. Don't ya have a pretty lil lass you'd rather be with?"

"She would understand, *if* I could tell her any of this and if she wasn't having a Matt Damon marathon with her Grams."

Pivoting in his seat, Cal turned to face me. "Is this a gay thing? Are ya feelin' an attraction here and don't know how tah handle it? I appreciate that mate. I do. You are a very attractive man. I can admit that. But I jus' don't have those inklings. If I did," Caleb clapped his hand on my knee, "I'm sure I would be honored by yer affections."

"You would be so lucky." Drumming my fingers against the table, I sized this alternate Caleb up and found him lacking. "You want the truth, college boy? I think you've been hurting people, be it consciously or in some sort of Freddy Krueger dream state way. Either way, I fully intend to make sure from this point on you are as docile as a fluffy little bunny."

Cal dragged his palm over his mouth, his expression darkening. "You think me tah be this horrible beast, yet yah believe ya'r mere presence could tame me? What kind of monster could be squelched so easily?"

Our eyes locked, daring the other to look away.

On the table between us, my phone vibrated to life, dancing across the table.

Neither of us looked away, but allowed it to shimmy.

Caleb's mouth tugged back in an arrogant smirk, one raven brow hiked in question. "Are ya gonna get that?"

Cursing under my breath, I tore my stare away to glance at my phone. Celeste's name illuminated the screen.

Snatching it off the table, I pointed the contraption at the possibly possessed bloke. "I'm going to take this. *You* don't kill anyone while I'm gone."

Scooping up his beer, Cal tipped it in my direction. "I will do my best."

Dissatisfied, I stabbed my phone in Red's direction. "*You*, watch him!"

Red glanced up from his plate of hot wings with wide eyes. "*Mmpherify*?"

"Like you never have before," I responded, and tapped the accept button.

"*She's making sexy noises!*" my phone shrieked.

"Talk me through it, pet." With one finger in my opposite ear, I dodged around a mysterious pile—which looked like chowder but smelled like vomit—in search of a more conversation friendly area.

On the other end, Celeste sighed in that way that I knew made her chest swell invitingly. "We're watching the Bourne movies—the good ones, before Hawkeye—and every time Matt Damon appears, Grams makes sex noises. *I shouldn't know what her sexy time noises sound like, Row! That is not information I should have!*"

"You lived with your Grams for years, and she's a very ..." *choose your words carefully, pirate,* "*free* woman. Surely this can't be the first time she's been open about such things?"

Silence.

"Did you just call my grandmother easy?" my beloved one asked. FYI, guys, such a question is a trap that will lead to days on end of misery. Lucky for me, I was centuries old and had played these games before.

"Heavens no! The woman is one step away from saint-hood!" I yelled over the guitar twangs of the band warming up for their set. "I just meant free with her feelings and emotions, which is an admirable trait that I aspire to myself.”

One should wear boots when slinging shit that deep.

“I know you’re full of crap, but at this point I don’t even care.” Celeste sighed. “What time is guys’ night wrapping up? I need to be spared from the ickiness.”

Stretching out my hunched back, I glanced to the table.

Caleb was gone.

“I’ll be there when I can,” I mumbled, killing the call with my thumb.

Shoving my way through the crowd, I slammed my palms on the table hard enough to make Red’s hot wings jump. “*Where is he*?”

He gaped up with a face full of sauce. “H-he was just there,” he stammered.

“Did *any* of you see which direction the alleged murderer went?” posed the question to the ceiling, the mere sight of the incompetent band fillin me with desire to go on my own bloody rampage.

Eddie and Beard Face tore their attentions away from the trivia game o the overhead screen. Lone Twin paused in his endless quest to flag down th waitress—poor lad hadn’t been able to score himself even a glass of water thu far. Between them, they exchanged cringes at their ineptitude.

“I think there’s a chance he may have followed a leggy blonde out. Lone Twin grimaced, his shoulders rising to his ears.

Throwing my hands in the air, I let them slap to my sides i exasperation. “I blame myself for trusting demons. Our kind can be distracte by a rash of violence or a tinfoil ball. In all of your bumbling incompetence, di you happen to notice *which way he went*?”

Swallowing hard, he pointed in the direction of the back door.

Before his hand could fall, I forced my way through the pub's cloud of eer burps and musky sexual frustration to the clearly marked back exit. The wind ripped the door from my grasp the second I forced it open, lashing against ny skin in warning for me to turn back. A chilling soundtrack of screams ssaulted my ears, riding back on the galloping breeze:

The unmistakable ruckus of a scuffle.

Choked gurgles rising in a distressed feminine throat.

A distressed male voice, with a recognizable brogue, shouted, *"Get way from her!"*

Falling into a defensive posture, I spun in time to see the flash of blonde rom a body being thrown against the brick façade of the neighboring nail salon. lesh dragged over unforgiving stone as the whimpering lass was yanked down nd bent backwards over a dumpster by an enormous figure in a dingy gray oodie.

Caleb pounded his fists into the back and sides of the shadowed figure, ith all the strength the mortal limitations he imposed upon himself would llow. The entity didn't so much as pause. Shoulders swelling like a dog raising s hackles, it leaned over the flailing girl. From where I stood, I could see the utline of its jaw stretching out wide in a maw no human could achieve. Her noked cries reached a fevered plateau, legs kicking in desperation of freedom.

Tipping my head, I dove into the beast's mind, immediately slamming to an impenetrable fortress of darkness. Pain, with the force of a railroad ike being drove into my frontal lobe, knocked me to my knees. An anguished ream tore from my throat. Blinking to clear my blurring vision, I glanced up to e the girl's body spastically convulsing. In a flurry of snorts and slobbery nomps, the hound drew an ethereal mist from his victim's gaping mouth that I uld only assume to be her soul.

"We have tah do something! *Help me!*" Caleb screamed to be heard over the torrential gusts that kicked up, mirroring his frantic emotions.

Rising on unsteady legs, I toed the gray area that comes with having a villainous history and hung back. A hero would have joined Cal and pounded on the beast until their fists were bloody in hopes of saving the girl. Maybe it was my loose morals talking, but I saw that for the pointless waste it was. My alternative took me into the mind of the fading blonde. There I applied pressure to her waning consciousness.

"Go to sleep. That's a girl. You deserve a little siesta," I coached.

One final whimper escaped her before she relented, her limbs sagging limp in her spiral into the comforts of the welcoming oblivion. With the sleeping lass out of the way, I settled into the driver's seat of her controls. Using her hands, I grabbed the beast by the shoulders and smashed her knee hard into its groin. It stumbled back a half-step, allowing me to shuffle her forward to collapse in Caleb's waiting arms.

"Jenna? Can you hear me, lass?" Brushing the hair back from her face uncharacteristic fear wavered through Cal's tone. It reminded me of how truly alone I was in this fight. Unless, of course, my former mate picked that particular moment to regain his memory and morph into the raging Titon fought beside countless times. That would be a swell development. Unfortunately, judging by the sheen of nervous sweat dotting his forehead and upper lip, this would not be the case.

Bulging muscles, which lined the hound's back, visibly prickled beneath stretched cotton fabric.

"The pirate …" it rasped, an ominous chortle quaking its brawny shoulders. "I hadn't planned on us meeting quite yet."

"If it's a meet and greet you're after, let's send the riffraff home and get to it." Rocking back on my heels, I hooked my thumbs in my front pockets and assumed a wide-legged stance.

"Take them," the beast snarled as if describing discarded candy wrappers. "They were merely a distraction until I got *your* attention."

"Get her out of here," I calmly ordered Caleb, my gaze never wavering from the broad back of the beast.

Gathering Jenna in his arms, uncertainty carved deep lines of worry into Cal's brow.

"Go!" I barked, my tone an iron clad stamp of resolve.

"I'll be back, brotha," Caleb promised, and hurried off with Jenna's head bobbing against the crook of his arm.

"*Did you like my gift*?" the Hellhound rumbled. With its hood raised I could gather no clues about its identity other than its formidable size—which was an attribute that described more than half of the Demonic-American community. Still, something about its stature and mannerisms struck a note of familiarity. "*I wrapped her just for you*."

"I admit to being a bit thick-headed at times," I said with a cocky smirk I truly wasn't feeling, "but even *I* was able to pick up on that less than subtle gesture, yes."

"*She begged for mercy and cried out each time I tasted her*," that menacing vibrato crooned. "*With a hand to her throat, I soothed her by relaying how crucial she was in delivering my message*."

Turning my façade of indifference up a notch, I ran one hand over the back of my neck and peered up from under my brow. "And what message would that be?"

Slowly and deliberately, the barge-like frame turned my way.

Topaz eyes locked with mine, crinkling in amusement at the shock that registered on my face.

And it did.

I needed no reflective surface to know my complexion had drained tc the ashen hue of white caps on harsh waves.

My vision tunneled.

The beating of my heart drowned out all other sound.

"A warning ... to stay away from my sister," Gabe snarled, his lips curling from his teeth to reveal jagged canine incisors.

Gone was the noble lion sentry. The meat suit stalking the width of the alley before me seemed more monster than man. Salvia dripped from his fangs His swollen brow puckered into deep slashes between his eyes, plunging ou into a narrow wolf-snout.

"The fun is just beginning, and I have good games for all," Gab growled, his shoulders rolling with predatory intent. *"I'll be seeing* you *rea soon."*

Leaping into the air with inhuman grace, he bounded back and fort from one building to the other. Repelling higher and higher, he crested th pub's rooftop and vanished into the night.

CHAPTER 8

"I warned you never to return!" Malise's jaws snapped inches from my ace.

With both arms mashed to her chest, I struggled against her. My notivation? Preventing row after row of her razor sharp teeth from shredding ny flesh to the bone.

Solidifying in her grotto, I interrupted combat training between her and er guard. Still, her face splitting into a wide, carnivorous maw hell-bent on evouring me seemed a bit of an over-reaction.

"Valid point." Back pressed against the rocky cavern wall, I did my best o pretend I didn't see bits of whale flesh lodged between her teeth, or the ccosting smell accompanying it.

In their relaxed form, mermaids were the most beguiling creatures ever o grace the earth. Rile them up, and they were the stuff of watery nightmares.

"As a counterpoint," forcing the words through my teeth, I pushed away om her with all my might, "have you ever considered a *Do Not Disturb* sign as pposed to devouring your unwanted guests? I mean, you have no idea where ve been. How do you know I'll even sit well?"

Gums rolling back with a shark-like quality, she retracted her jagged eeth into folds of flesh along her jawline until only their human-looking ounterparts remained.

"Why would you risk coming back here?" She glowered, her pert nose urling in a snarl. "And make the answer convincing, lest I get *peckish*."

"I need more information on Hellhounds," I stated, straightening my fish-scented shirt.

Expelling an aggravated sigh, she reluctantly released me. Spinning away, her shoulders sagged.

"There's nothing more to say." Scooping up the sword that clanged to the ground when she attacked me, Malise turned it one way then the other to inspect it for damage. "Find the beast, and kill it before it spreads and forms a pack. It's really a matter of simple mathematics. One Hellhound is easier to manage than an enraged mass of them."

With a nod to her beefy guard, they resumed their land-bound exercises. Metal clapped together with each lobbed strike.

"What if I can't … kill it?" I stammered, my own unease making me painfully aware of the stifling humidity in that stuffy space. "There has to be some *other* way to stop it."

Malise paused mid-lunge. Head tilted, her eyes narrowed to leery slits. "This isn't a beast you can tame and keep as a pet. It is a *plague* with fangs. Wh then—with all the dastardly things you've done, and all the people you've kille and betrayed—are you even hesitating?"

My tongue dragged over my top teeth, hating the vile taste of the word before they even formed. "He's her brother."

Head falling forward, a curtain of flaxen waves veiled Malise's face a she rested the tip of her blade against the stone floor and chuckled softly. "Ah yes. The proverbial '*she*' that can be found at the root of almost any problem, c idea. And for her happiness you wish to spare her kin?"

Knowing that to be the short and simple version of a much longe conundrum, I bobbed my head side to side in a vague, non-committal fashion "In a matter of speaking. What, then, can be done? You must know c alternatives."

“Leave us,” the mer-queen commanded to her subject over her narrow shoulder.

Listening to the drumming chorus of water that dripped from a crack in he wall, we waited for the merman to leap head-first into the hot spring. His ail slapped the water, dotting my boots with droplets.

Only then did she peer my way once more, her intensity fixed and nwavering. Hand slipping from her hilt, she dropped the sword. Metal onnected with the ground in an echoing clang that bounced off each wall. Vetting her succulent lips, Malise prowled my way. Closing the distance etween us with an alluring sashay, the shells of her bra caught and snagged the abric of my shirt. Swallowing hard, I forced myself to stand firm—but not erect. *hem*. Backing away, or acknowledging her charms with so much as a lifted row would be perceived a display of weakness I couldn’t allow.

Her gaze traced the curve of my mouth as if hypnotized by the memory f it.

“You can wriggle into the minds of others, make them feel what you feel nd think what you think. You draw things out of them they didn’t know iemselves capable of.” The warmth of her breath tickled over my cheek, her ottom lip teasing against mine. The whole event would’ve been far more nticing if I wasn’t in love with another woman, and if the figure before me adn’t tried to eat me alive mere moments ago. “Utilize that talent. Coax the arkness from the brother and into another vessel you can kill, or control.”

Grinding my teeth, I mulled over the options at my disposal—a college ll of them, in fact. The notion was compelling, despite its one enormous flaw. can’t get into his mind. I tried. It’s like he has a force field of evil protecting m. No, I can do better than that. A malicious cocoon? Malevolent shell? I can’t ink of a good metaphor while your breasts are touching me.”

Tracing her fingers down my arm with a chuckle that screamed of sin, she caused an outbreak of goose bumps wherever her chilled flesh touched mine. "You don't go *in*. You lure him *out* with the promise of a swap so tempting he couldn't possibly refuse it. You're a clever boy, Rowan. I have no doubt you can wrangle such a prize. Even so, I have to ask, how do you think this lady of yours will react when she learns you sacrificed one innocent life for another? Will your act of chivalry tarnish you in her eyes forever?"

Breathing in the sudden epiphany of what needed to be done, I exhaled my vile truth through pursed lip.

"For once," I rasped, "I think it's *exactly* what she would expect from me."

Celeste flung the door open with her shoes on and bag already slung over her shoulder. "'Kay, bye! Going to the flimaninarty!"

The three remaining Garrett women barely glanced up from their TV, phone, or pregnancy book distractions. The pajama clad trio dismissed her with incoherent mumblings and half-hearted waves.

"Flimaninarty?" I asked.

Pulling the door shut behind her, Celeste leaned her back against it. "They had a fifty-four minute—and, yes, I timed it—discussion on why Matt Damon's character in *The Martian* would be the perfect man. Something about two years on a planet alone making him an attentive listener. Around the twenty minute marker, I began plotting this social experiment to prove they are the *worst* listeners on the planet. Flimaninarty is my ironic victory."

“We will have to celebrate accordingly.” Catching the strings of her Rhodes College hoodie, I drew her in for a quick taste of her lips. “First, where’s your brother?”

“I was hoping we could do this without him.”

Reluctantly pulling back, my stare pleaded for the answer.

Mouth curling to the side, her chestnut eyes rolled skyward. “Alaina was feeling nauseous. He went to get her some ginger tea and pregnancy pops. Follow up question, why does your shirt smell like a tackle box?”

“I went fishing for answers.” Lacing my fingers into the hair at the base of her scalp, I gave a gentle tug.

Body molding to mine, her lips parted in an open invitation. “Did you find what you were looking for?”

“I did, the first time I saw you smile.” Crushing my mouth to hers, I lost myself in salty-sweet bliss.

Curling into me, she moaned her appreciation. My wandering fingers traveled from her shoulder blades to the subtle curve of her hips. Lips never parting, our hammering hearts beat a steady chorus of mutual urgency.

Breath coming in ragged pants, I squeezed my eyes shut and pressed my forehead to hers. “I thought just being with you would be enough,” trapping a lock of her hair between two fingers, I twirled the silky strands from my knuckles to fingertips, “but I need to know it’s real.”

Catching my hand in both of hers, Celeste took a step back. A blend of confusion and concern puckered her brow. “What are you talking about? Of course it is.” A quiver of betraying nerves sullied her laugh.

Begrudging the distance between us, I linked my fingers with hers. Everything I’ve done in my life; the trials I faced, the strumpets I’ve fancied ...”

“Not loving this story so far.”

Raising her hand, I dotted a kiss to the inside of her wrist. "It's all made me who I am today: a broken, shell of a man loving you the only way he knows how."

Her expression a question mark, she searched my face for answers. "Did you steal one of Kendall's Nicholas Sparks books? Because I don't speak chick lit. I'm going to have to get her out here to translate this into sardonic quips."

I huffed with laughter despite the situation. "I need you to know … *ugh*! I don't even know what the hell I need you to know!"

Lips curling in a downward C, Celeste let her shoulders rise and fall. "In that case, we're on the same page here."

Grumbling my frustration, I stepped forward and cradled her face between my palms. The flecks of gold swirling in her molasses eyes beckoned me home with the clarity of the Northern Star. "I want you to know that your happiness is the most important thing to me. Any obstacles that threaten to destroy that, I will remove in any manner necessary … because I love you."

"I thought *love* was too overused a word for your taste?"

"Sometimes it's the only one that works."

Our lips found each other with a passion that left us both breathless. Fa too soon, with the sharpened claws of anguish ripping my heart to shreds, I expelled myself from the haven of her embrace.

"Flimaninarty will have to wait, with my promise that we will define it ir the sauciest way possible the very next time we're together." After breathing the words into her, I turned on my heel and strode away from the woman I loved.

"Rowan!" she called after me.

I paused, tipping my chin her way without looking back.

"*Mo chroi*, I've heard that somewhere before. What is it?"

"It's you, Celeste, *my heart*."

CHAPTER 9

One rap on the cracked and faded door of Caleb's loft, and he threw it ›pen as if he'd been waiting just inside. While he gaped in shock that I tracked ›im down—*hello, I can delve into the minds of others, not really a challenge here*—I got straight to the point. "The blonde lass, is she okay?"

Caleb glanced protectively over his shoulder. "Aye, she's restin' now. ›oor thing will have questions when she wakes that I can't answ'r."

"That sounds like *Future Caleb's* problem. Right now, I'm gonna need *'resent Caleb* to come with me." Grabbing him by the collar of his crisp black T-hirt, I yanked him out the door. In a churning cloud I whisked us both back to ›e alley of the attack.

"Blimey! What the blazes was that?" Cal asked, his pallor morphing to ›e same green hue of his eyes. Hands on his knees, he tried to breathe through ›e off-putting vertigo that accompanies teleportation.

"Oh, where are we, wha's happenin'?" I quipped in my worst, and most ›prechaun-esque impression of him. Loose gravel crunching under my boots, I ›oved my hands in the pockets of my coat to fight off the nip of night. "Even in › alternate reality, you're still *frightfully* predictable."

Caleb spun at the sound of my voice, his gaze locking on the spot in the ley where the hound attempted to feast on his date. "How did we get here? 'ho are you? And, *most importantly*, what the bloody hell was that thing?" he ›manded, the magnitude of his snit making him oblivious to my snark. "That ›as like nothin' I've e'er seen before!"

Eyebrows raised, I held up one finger to correct him. "That's not entirely true. You've seen that, and far worse, you just don't remember."

Caleb jabbed one hand at the space the Hellhound had occupied, as if a trace of it still lingered there. "*That* is not the kind of thing you forget!"

"Oh, yes!" Pantomiming glee, I clapped my hands in front of me. "Let's waste time by playing Memory! Wait … there's a killer beast on the loose, isn't there? Drat. We'll have to stop that first, *then* we can braid each other's hair and catch up. How's that sound?"

Caleb's mouth twisted in annoyance. "Like you really enjoy the sound of ya'r own voice. Has anyone e'er finished a conversation with you and *not* wanted to punch ya in the throat by the end?"

"My nana." I nodded, then cocked my head as I reconsidered. "Wait … that's not true. Nana had a wicked right hook."

Shaking his head in annoyance, a lock of raven hair fell across Caleb's forehead. "As fun as your little quips are—for you, I mean, society told me to tell you ya'r a pain in the arse—I want to know how we stop that thing."

"You're willing to help?" I ventured, holding my breath in anticipation of his answer.

"Absolutely. What do ya need from me?" Boy scout that he was, Caleb easily slid into the role of the hero … as I hoped he would.

"What do I need from you?" Biting the inside of my cheek, I pivoted on my heel and paced the width of the alley. "Well, these matters always come down to a girl. Don't they, mate?"

"The brunette from the pub?"

"Aye. Her name is Celeste, and what I need from you now," halting directly in front of him, I clapped one hand onto his broad shoulder, "is for you to remember her."

Focusing my attentions, I dove into Caleb's mind. Immediately, I umped into the wall constructed there. Since many of you probably haven't ad the good fortune of roaming through another person's mind, allow me to aint a picture of the landscape of that amazing realm. Every memory, every car, every moment of true bliss creates another woven thread in the intricate apestry of each individual thinker. It's a glorious collection of flaws. Anticipating hat and finding the perfect, unblemished blockade protecting Caleb's brain rom the truth, made it that much more foreign and off-putting.

Exploring its surface, I measured it for imperfections. Finding a nick here and a bulge here, I located one protruding memory ... and pushed. Teeth lenched, body trembling with the strain, my cognizance struck with all the orce I could muster, and the wall came tumbling down.

It only took a beat.

Clarity sharpened Caleb's gaze, his features morphing with a dangerous dge.

"*You rotten bastard,*" he growled through his teeth.

Balling his hands into flaming fists, he snapped my head back with a erce uppercut. Skin crackled, the cartilage of my nose crunched. Still, I had it oming.

"You had your memories this entire time!" he bellowed, his face orphing from red to purple. "And you used them to manipulate her! She's not a'r toy, Rowan! She's a *person*, one you used fer ya'r own pleasures!"

Running my tongue over my teeth, I spat out the blood-tinged saliva at filled my mouth with a coppery rush. "And if *you* had the opportunity, you ould've done the exact same thing. You would've moved mountains to make er fall for that *fine Irish façade* all over again. You're just pissy I beat you to it."

"*Did you sleep with her*?" he demanded. Every tendon of his neck bulging, he took a threatening step toward me. "*Did you* actually *take it that far*?"

"Come now, how is knowing that calling her *My Queen* makes her long for a slap on the ass going to help this matter?" Feigning shock, I covered my mouth with one hand. "Oops ... I've said too much."

"I *will* kill you for this, Rowan. Consider that my vow tah you." Fire blazed in his eyes, promising. He meant every word.

Staring passed him, my body stiffened.

"For the moment, you may need to take a number and get in line," pointed out, jerking my chin down the alleyway. "We've got company."

Caleb followed my gaze. His body tensed, just as mine had, to see Gabe's ominous frame filling the back entrance to the narrow aisle. Puffing hi cheeks, Cal exhaled through puckered lips. "When my memories came back they brought with them the gruesome knowledge of these beasts an' what the can do. I really hope you have a plan."

Glancing at him out of the corner of my eye, I threw one hand in the air "*Where would be the fun in that*?"

"They both come to defend her honor," the Gabe-hound boomed from the far side of the alley. Chest rising and falling in heaving pants, saliva dripped from his fangs. "How livid she would be to learn of that."

Caleb's arms pulled from his sides, poised for battle.

I took a slightly different approach, my hands meeting in front of me i a cavalier snap/clap. With a playful gait that could have easily transitioned into skip, I approached the beast with blood red eyes and a less than cheer disposition.

"I suppose you have gotten to know her during all this time posing as ner loving brother," I commented in a conversational manner. "Tell me, why oother? Why not just devour all their souls while they slept?"

Gabe's head cocked, his inner hound perking one curious ear. "The one vho calls me *babe* is with child. There is no soul sweeter than that of an nnocent newborn."

"You hear that, Cal?" I called over my shoulder. "He's playing the doting husband so he can *eat the baby*. That's dedication to a goal, right there. A truly admirable tenacity."

"I can name four words ya used wrong in that statement alone," Caleb nuttered, slowly creeping up behind me.

He was following. *Good*.

"Is any of the meathead brother left in there?" Crouching down, then ising up on tiptoe, I made great show out of examining every lumpy, bumpy idge of Gabe's face and torso.

Recoiling at my intimate proximity, foam bubbled in the corners of the east's mouth. "He's here, but not strong enough to resist my influence. Few re."

"Of course they can't," I erupted. Slapping my hand on his bulging bicep, gave it a friendly squeeze that made his torso reverberate in a vicious growl. Look at you! You're a heaving beast! If only you had a more worthy receptacle, nagine what you could do ..."

"Rowan, what are you doing?" Caleb whispered, speaking directly to my etter judgment.

The Hellhound's shoulders puffed in offense. "What is wrong with my eceptacle? It kills with ease and agility!"

"As it should! It's a lovely ... package," I agreed, cringing at my own less than stellar word choice. "But, you know, it's *human*. It's only capable of so much. Had you picked a *demon,* you'd have their fun little talents to play with."

"My receptacle has been chosen," the hound snorted, shaking the thought off with a canine toss of his head. "It cannot be undone."

Keeping one hand planted on him, I tossed the other one out in a wide gesture. "Of course it can, mate! With the right help, and—here's your fun prize with purchase—there just so happens to be *two* chaps infected with demon blood right in front of you. Handsome human packaging with none of that bothersome weakness or mortality!"

Caleb halted where he stood, icy awareness sagging his shoulders and dilating his pupils to ink-black pits. "You filthy basta'd. This is why you wanted me here, tah sacrifice me to yar mongrel."

"Shhh! Don't ruin the ending," I taunted, one finger pressed to my lips. "You'll kill the suspense of it."

The Gabe-hound eyed Caleb as if he were a shiny new sports car he couldn't wait to slide behind the wheel of—in a *mostly* hetero way.

"What powers does he have?" he asked, dragging his lolling tongue over his teeth.

"Rowan, no," Caleb warned, attempting a step in retreat. "You don't have to do this."

Head listing to the side, I applied my gift and halted him where he stood. "He possesses the blood of a Titan, meaning he can control the four elements. Produce fire from the palms of his hands, tremble the earth, create wind storm, and ... *uh* ... something pertaining to water. Anywho, a far more entertaining prospect than a human sack of deteriorating flesh."

"I came here to kill you, Rowan Wade," the hound stated in more fact than threat. "That's been my goal since the Countess branded this receptacle and called me forth. Fortunately for you, if you can make such a transition possible, I *would* consider sparing you."

"Blimey, Rowan! You can't trust *a Hellhound*! Release me an' we can fight this thing togetha!"

"I have mind control abilities," I batted the words away with a flick of my wrist, belittling their value. "A bothersome trait, really. However, in this nstance it's quite useful. I can lure your essence out of one form and guide it ight into the other."

The hound's hackles rose, his expansive back arching in outrage. "*And ow do I know you won't attempt to vanquish me when I leave this form*?"

Fighting to keep my expression neutral, I offered him a tight-lipped mile. "Well, mate, not that you aren't *charming* company, but if I knew how to anquish you, we wouldn't be having this conversation."

"If you try to betray me, I will yank your spinal cord out your mouth and hove it up your ass," the Gabe-hound warned, shifting his weight anxiously rom one foot to the other.

"I met a girl in Singapore that could do a similar trick. It involved a far ifferent bone though." Peering up at him, I offered him my most beguiling mile. "So, what do you say? Do we have an accord?"

The beast didn't verbally relent, but snorted his agreement.

That was what I wanted, what I planned for. Even so, the victory came ashing in on a tide of melancholy.

"This may sting a bit," I warned the hound, centering myself to the task t hand.

"Row, why are you doing this?" Caleb, the little cartoon cricket of my onscious, asked with disappointment slathering each word.

"Every day that I was with her, holding her in my arms, I fell a little more love. And every day I became more and more aware that it was never real.

Why?" I pondered, rambling on before he could answer. "Because, I wasn't with the *real* Celeste. All I had to hold on to was the shadow of her left behind from the Gryphon's spell."

"And ya'r plan is to … what? Remove the competition from the equation so I don't louse things up for ya?" Caleb spat in disgust.

Pausing, I offered him a sad smile, then cerebrally reached for the hound's essence. This time, it reached back, welcoming me to the roaring bedlam and cravings for gore within. Coaxing, urging, and persuading his wil with every trick I possessed, I lured it from its heaving form.

"Celeste needs a man that is worthy of her," with beads of swea sprouting across my forehead, I uttered the declaration to Caleb as much as myself. "Someone who would make *any* needed sacrifice without batting ar eye."

"You *know* her," Caleb countered, pushing against my influence for us of leaden limbs. "Sacrificin' anotha fer yar own needs will *only* turn her agains you!"

Wrangling the twisting darkness, it lashed out at me with unsee slashes. Its hunger for change quickly whipping into a frenzy.

"Celeste will understand … in time." Forcing the words through m locked jaws, sweat streamed down my back and soaked my shirt. Slapping hand on Gabe's shoulder, I pulled back with all my might, extracting the las remnants of his demonic infection. Wind kicked up in a cyclone around me, m hair whipping my cheeks raw. *"I'm doing this for her!"*

Gabe slumped to his knees, head falling back like a loose PEZ dispense A geyser of crimson fog gushed from his lips, vacating its spent vessel.

"She won't see it that way, brotha," Caleb shouted, his chest puffe with a warrior's bravado. *"You do this and you will lose her fore'er."*

Toppling sideways, Gabe crashed to the ground, his chest rising and falling in shallow pants. In his place hovered a blood red mass of rolling and writhing energy. Lost in its hypnotic pull, I noticed tiny bolts of lightning zagging and planking from one cloud-like tuft to another.

"Rowan, don't do this!" Caleb desperately thrashed for freedom.

"I *am* sorry. You need to know that. If I could think of any other way ..." Tearing my stare from the mesmerizing inevitable, I looked to my *true* first mate for what I feared would be the last time. "Someone that knows the true atrocities of this world needs to be here to protect her. To keep her away from all of it, so she can squeeze out every bit of happiness she has earned. That someone is *you*, Caleb."

In a blink, confusion snuffed out the inferno of rage sweltering in Caleb's emerald glare. "*Me*? Row, are ya daft?"

Throwing my arms out wide, I opened myself to that foul shadow.

"Keep her safe, Cal. Take care of her!" I screamed to be heard over the crackles of swarming electricity. It snaked and coiled around me, eager to stake its claim. *"Find Terin! Unleash the Phoenix!"*

"Row, stop! We can find another way! Don't do this!" Cal begged, stumbling forward a step as my influence wavered.

Malice cocooned me, building and brewing into a stifling fortress. Lifting my chin, I rose on tiptoe to deliver one final message before it consumed me. "Whatever happens, Cal ... *Keep her away from me!"*

The hound's life-force seeped through my pores, invaded every orifice. I found myself sinking into the tarry blackness, dragged down to the depths of dormancy and locked away there.

I wouldn't know until the next time I peered into a mirror, at a face I didn't recognize, of the physical changes that accompanied the hijacking. The dull pallor of ash that coated my golden strands. My complexion, formerly sun-kissed to a warm tan, drained to flawless porcelain. I refocused on the world, not with my usual charming sapphire gaze, but with a maniacal stare of rubies encircled by onyx.

At the muffled sound of something scrapping across the ground, I twisted my head to see Gabe struggling to his knees.

Hands falling to his sides, the eldest Garrett peered up at me with a blend of terror and pity. "Rowan, *what have you done*?"

A veil seemed to separate me from the world, its opaque cloak detaching me from the urgency of the living.

"He upgraded," a raspy growl reverberated my chest, yet I hadn't spoken a word.

The Hellhound had control.

In my foggy state I tried to remember why I cared.

"*Rowan*!" Body moving without my consent, I spun in Caleb's direction. My head tilted in interest. "I know ya'r still in there! Fight it, brotha! Ya'r one of the strongest blokes I know! *Take control!"*

The hound's chuckle dripped with malicious intent. *"That* had *been his plan. He thought he could suppress me, keep me locked away like a mongrel pup. And for what? To be the noble hero to a worthless meat-sack*?"

"He's doing it for me, and I won't let him!" Rising on visibly unsteady legs, Gabe pulled himself to up to full height. "Take me. I'll willingly turn myself over, *if* you spare the pirate."

"Well," the hound scoffed, pacing a slow, predatory circle around Gabe, "didn't I find myself in the den of champions. Each so willing to throw themselves on the proverbial sword. That being the case, I have to ask why you think I would *ever* disregard this shell for yours? This one is positively dripping with power."

Gabe's barrel chest puffed with pride. "Because I remember who I am now ..."

Locked deep within my own body, I shook my head and pounded my fists, screaming for him to stop. My cries went unheard.

"... and I know what I can do."

"Noooo!" Caleb's hand shot out, as if to halt the unavoidable.

A gesture too little, too late.

Falling on all fours, Gabe's form shifted in a gruesome display of cracks and pops. Hair sprouted. Fangs elongated. Claws curled into the earth. In the end, the majestic lion emerged. Tossing his mane, he threw his head back and unleashed a mighty roar into the Tennessee night sky.

His *own* otherworldly elements awakened, Caleb called fire to him once again. Flames engulfed the length of his arms in orange and yellow tendrils, licking from his flesh. "Gabe, get behind me! *Now!"*

The lion didn't run or cower. Instead, he laid down in a submissive offering before the Hellhound, before ... *me*.

I could feel the hound's giddy delight, taste his brewing bloodlust, and I struggled against it with all I had.

"Tsk, tsk, tsk," the hound clucked, running my hand over my chin. "Isn't this a fascinating development? The Guardian to the Gryphon's Conduit, which can only mean somewhere in your little circle of friends awaits the fated Chosen One. That is utterly *delicious*."

My treacherous hand lashed out in a blur of speed, connecting with the base of the lion's skull. The potent strike drove him to the ground, severing his spine in a gruesome crunch of bone. His massive head fell to the side at an unnatural angle; feline eyes fixed and dilated.

As I watched in horror, the lion sentry morphed back into the Gabe's lifeless body.

The Garrett clan's first fallen soldier.

Fighting against my prison, I scrambled and scrapped to regain control.

"*What's the matter, pirate*?" the hound shouted, his gruff vibratc echoing down the alley. "Sad to see your last heroic effort rendered utterly pointless? *What did you think would happen when you deceived me*? You promised me the Titan!" Spinning on Caleb, I felt my lip curl from my teeth in a threatening snarl. "If I can't have him, I'll just have to turn him! It's time I begin building my pack."

Caleb's fiery arms rose defensively, his glare screaming for vengeance.

For a moment, I punched my way through—forcing back the curtain or a fleeting instant of clarity.

"Caleb, I've got him! *Run!*"

"*Gabe!*" he hollered, gaze flicking to the heaped form.

The hound clawed and scratched for the surface, desperate to drag me back down.

"It's too late, he's gone! I can't hold him, Cal! Go! Keep her safe!"

Caleb's flames extinguished. Wearing a mask of admiration, he clapped one hand over his heart. "I will find a way to save you, brotha. I promise you that."

As my hold slipped, tossing me back down the rabbit-hole of despair Caleb vanished in a puff of black.

Instead of giving chase, the hound threw his head back in a wicked cackle.

"Let them *all* run and hide," he growled. "I *will* find them ... find *her*. Then, dear Rowan, I will make great sport of playing with your beloved. Her screams for mercy will be the last thing you hear as you watch your *own hand* wring the life from her body."

TO BE CONTINUED ...

THE GRYPHON SERIES RESURRECTION
continues with
INFERNO
Fall of 2016!

About the Author

RONE Award Winner for Best YA Paranormal Work of 2012 for Embrace, a Gryphon Series Novel
Young Adult and Teen Reader voted Author of the Year 2012
Turning Pages Magazine Winner for Best YA book of 2013 & Best Teen Book of 2013
Readers' Favorite Silver Medal Winner for Crane 2015

Stacey Rourke is the author of the award winning YA Gryphon Series, the chillingly suspenseful Legends Saga, and the romantic comedy Adapted for Film. She lives in Michigan with her husband, two beautiful daughters, and two giant dogs. She loves to travel, has an unhealthy shoe addiction, and considers herself blessed to make a career out of talking to the imaginary people that live in her head.

Visit her at www.staceyrourke.com
diaryofasemi-crazyauthor.blogspot.com
Facebook at www.facebook.com/staceyrourkeauthor
or on Twitter or Instagram @Rourkewrites

Printed in Poland
by Amazon Fulfillment
Poland Sp. z o.o., Wrocław